"So," she said when he remained silent. "Are you going to help me find them?"

"You can rest assured that I'll find them, MJ. You needn't doubt that for a moment."

"So far so good."

"But you won't be accompanying me on my search, tagging along like a—" He broke off. He was a civilized man. He refused to descend to insults.

Those damned eyes danced again, reminding him of a shady inlet on his grandfather's Greek island, the sea dancing in the sun as a breeze ruffled its surface. "Were you going to say like a piece of unwanted baggage...or a bad smell... Thorn in your side, perhaps?"

Whatever she saw in his face had her throwing back her head and laughing. He shifted. He didn't understand this woman at all.

She swiped her fingers beneath her eyes, her merriment slowly fading. "That, however, is not such excellent news." She cocked her head to one side. "I could be an asset, you know?"

Dear Reader,

Once in a blue moon the muse hands a writer a story that feels like an absolute gift. The characters spring to immediate life almost fully formed, and their goals and the reasons they want those things feel so real and matter so much, while their conflicts are heart-wrenchingly authentic. It starts to feel as if the book is writing itself.

That's what happened with MJ and Nikos's story. I'd been mulling over the story themes that I hadn't so far written and realized that while I'd written a lot of friends-to-lovers stories, I'd never written an enemies-to-lovers one. When I coupled it with feuding families and a hint of fated lovers, the story took off and it never looked back. Can you tell how much I loved writing this book?

I hope this story sweeps you away from the real world for a few happy hours, like it did for me, that MJ becomes your new best friend forever, like she did for me, and that Nikos makes your pulse pound a little bit harder. And I hope their journey to their happy-ever-after stays with you long after you finish the book.

Hugs and happy reading!

Michelle

Escape with Her Greek Tycoon

Michelle Douglas

Recycling programs
for this product may
not exist in your area.

ISBN-13: 978-1-335-40705-4

Escape with Her Greek Tycoon

Copyright © 2022 by Michelle Douglas

This edition published by arrangement with Harlequin Books S.A.

For questions and comments about the quality of this book,
please contact us at CustomerService@Harlequin.com.

Harlequin Enterprises ULC
22 Adelaide St. West, 41st Floor
Toronto, Ontario M5H 4E3, Canada
www.Harlequin.com

Printed in U.S.A.

Michelle Douglas has been writing for Harlequin since 2007 and believes she has the best job in the world. She lives in a leafy suburb of Newcastle, on Australia's east coast, with her own romantic hero, a house full of dust and books, and an eclectic collection of '60s and '70s vinyl. She loves to hear from readers and can be contacted via her website, michelle-douglas.com.

Books by Michelle Douglas

Harlequin Romance

A Baby in His In-Tray
The Million Pound Marriage Deal
Miss Prim's Greek Island Fling
The Maid, the Millionaire and the Baby
Redemption of the Maverick Millionaire
Singapore Fling with the Millionaire
Secret Billionaire on Her Doorstep
Billionaire's Road Trip to Forever
Cinderella and the Brooding Billionaire

Visit the Author Profile page
at Harlequin.com for more titles.

To Brad and Felicity, for the Friday night catch-ups, tea and whiskey, and weekend barbecues. The next round of orange whips are on us.

Praise for
Michelle Douglas

"Michelle Douglas writes the most beautiful stories, with heroes and heroines who are real and so easy to get to know and love.... This is a moving and wonderful story that left me feeling fabulous.... I do highly recommend this one, Ms. Douglas has never disappointed me with her stories."

—*Goodreads* on *Redemption of the Maverick Millionaire*

CHAPTER ONE

MJ PEERED AT the imposing façade of the Constantinos residence and blew out a breath. The
house was on Grosvenor Square in Mayfair, no
less. As if the Constantinos family was important landed gentry.

'This is the address, miss.'

The cab driver's voice made her start, but with
a quick smile she paid him before forcing herself
to step down to the footpath. The Constantinos
family might not be landed gentry but, whenever anything happened to remind her father of
where his sworn enemy lived, it was still a fact
that never failed to rile him. The current generation were 'only' second-generation British. She
shook her head. As if that made an ounce of difference to anything.

The Mabels, however, could trace their ances-
try back to the Restoration. Such things mattered
to her father—he was forever telling Siena and
her that they should be proud of such a heritage.
He wouldn't trade the family's Knightsbridge
mansion for any other property on the planet, but
the fact the Constantinos family lived in presti-
gious Grosvenor Square still rankled.

While MJ couldn't give a flying fig about how

far back a family could trace their ancestors or who lived where, she suspected it mattered just as much to Nikos Constantinos as it did to her father. And that meant she was the last person he'd be interested in helping.

'Which means the next half an hour is going to be fun,' she murmured as she marched up the stairs, seized the polished brass knocker—her father had one very like it in Knightsbridge—and rapped smartly on the dark door.

'Ms Mabel to see Mr Nikos Constantinos,' she said, sweeping past the butler into the grand foyer as if she were entitled to—as if she were the Queen herself. She had no intention of allowing the man to slam the door in her face or keep her ignominiously waiting on the doorstep.

'Is Mr Constantinos expecting you, Ms Mabel?'

'No, but assure him he will want to hear what I have to tell him.'

She planted herself on a hard-back chair and stared at him blandly, the picture of patience while still managing to emanate impatience. It had taken her a long time to perfect this particular attitude of entitlement. It made people edgy; made them clench their jaws and start to simmer. She rarely pulled it out of her arsenal, as it was mean-spirited, but she'd use every trick at her disposal today if she had to.

For a moment she thought he might lose his composure, but he was too well-trained. He inclined his head with a 'Very good, miss.' But his sniff told her he considered her presence in these hallowed halls a bad omen. She watched him stalk off down a hallway to the right. The direction of Nikos's study, no doubt.

She counted to twenty and then followed. Normally she'd never do anything so rude, but necessity was the mother of invention. And she wasn't leaving until she'd spoken to Nikos. Her stomach clenched. She couldn't fail. There was too much at stake.

You have time. There's still time.

Yeah, well, time had a habit of running out.

'If she wants to see me, tell her to make an appointment.'

There was no denying the hard, dark tones of Nikos Constantinos coming from the open doorway just up ahead. He had a voice threaded through with velvet and steel. She'd always found it rather attractive.

Not that she'd ever admit as much to a living soul.

She walked into his study with a confidence she was far from feeling, but in this instance it was better to show no weakness. 'How ungallant of you, Nikos. Rest assured, I won't take up much of your time. I believe you'll find what I have to say in your best interests to hear.'

His lips thinned. 'MJ, I presume?'

He was one of the few people who could tell her and Siena apart.

He waved away his man, who left on silent feet, closing the door behind him.

'Though, as you're actually dressed more like your sister, I can't help wondering if you were trying to fool me.'

'When you find out why I'm here, you'll realise what a stupid assumption that is.'

Her pale pink capri pants and flamingo print blouse had been a present from Siena. That was why she'd worn them today. She'd wanted—*needed*—to feel close to her twin.

His lips thinned even further. He hadn't stood when she'd entered the room—not that she could blame him, as he'd made it clear he didn't want her there—so she folded herself into the chair opposite his desk without an invitation. She had no intention of standing before him like a naughty child.

His lips twisted. 'Please, take a seat.'

'How kind of you.' But just for a moment she had to fight the urge to laugh at the absurdity of their barbed fake politeness.

He blinked, as if he'd read that impulse in her face, and then leaned towards her. She became aware of the tightly leashed masculinity contained in that impeccably cut business suit. Not that she was afraid he'd ever hurt her—not physically, anyway. 'What are you doing here, Marjorie? What do you want?'

She and Nikos had barely exchanged words one-on-one before. Oh, they moved in the same circles, attended many of the same parties and exchanged the briefest of courtesies when they happened upon each other in the interests of greasing the wheels of social intercourse. But that had always been in the presence of other people. She and Nikos had never actually been alone together before.

Well, except for that one time when she'd been sixteen, but that didn't count because *he* hadn't said anything. Oh, and there was that other time when she'd been nineteen, but it'd been in a noisy nightclub and they certainly hadn't been alone. She swallowed and pushed that particular memory as far from her mind as she could.

It was just…she'd always wondered how they'd address each another if—when—they finally did speak one-on-one. Her use of 'Nikos' had felt instinctive, while him calling her 'Marjorie'…

She swallowed. It sounded completely natural, but something about it made her mouth dry. Most people called her MJ, short for Marjorie Joan, including her father. Her twin called her Jojo. Nobody called her Marjorie. Did he hope to annoy her by using it? He'd be sadly disappointed, because she found she liked it. She liked the lilt in his voice when he said it.

For a moment she wished the two of them weren't sworn enemies. Suddenly the fake politeness, the pretence—the hate—wasn't funny. None of it was funny. Not in the slightest. She and Nikos didn't even know each other. You shouldn't hate someone you didn't know.

She lifted her chin. Well, she had every intention of ridding her family of that hate. But that wasn't the reason she was here today. She wished she could find a smile, wished she could be casual and confident. But face to face with him she couldn't feign any of those things. 'Why am I here and what do I want? Why, Nikos, I want your help.'

She half expected him to give one of those harsh, ugly, triumphant laughs her father was so adept at. He didn't. His eyebrows lifted and he eased back in his seat. 'And how, I wonder, do you think I can help you?'

At least it wasn't a straight-out *no*. But only because he was probably playing a deeper game— just as her father and his father before them had done. And his grandfather and her great-aunt before that. She bit back a sigh. Just because she didn't want to play this game any more, it didn't mean Nikos was of like mind. She'd be a fool to forget it. His questions would merely be an attempt to find a deeper and more damaging weakness, one he'd ruthlessly be able to exploit if he could.

So that he could ruin her family through her.

She refused to let her chin drop. 'My sister has gone missing. I want you to help me find her.'

He blinked, the surprise in his eyes quickly masked, but she'd been looking for it. She nodded gently. So he didn't know.

'Why do you think I should know where Siena is? And, even if I did, why do you think I would help you?'

Because she had something he desperately wanted.

'I don't think you do know, but Christian does. And I'm hoping you know how to find your little brother.'

Although it didn't look as if he'd moved a single muscle, everything about him grew harder, tighter and more forbidding. With his dark hair, dark eyes and olive skin, he looked like the Prince of Darkness himself.

She frowned. Except, his nose was a little bigger than the devil's would be if he were ever made flesh. It was certainly too large for perfection, but it added a certain stateliness to his face. It was a nose that had character. Perfection bored her. She had a feeling Nikos would never bore her.

She stamped the feminine appreciation flat. She might want to end two generations' worth of anger and resentment, but *that* wasn't going to happen.

Nikos and her an item? She couldn't imagine having an affair with someone she didn't trust. Oh, who was she trying to kid? Of course she could. She had a good imagination. It'd probably be terribly exciting—thrilling, even—but far from comfortable. She'd never be able to let her guard down.

She tried to shake off the weight that wanted to settle over her. If she succumbed to his charms, Nikos would chew her up and spit her out. She was pretty certain that wasn't the way to find the peace she so desperately sought for their families. Besides, the only thing she ought to be focusing on at the moment was finding Siena before her twin did irreparable damage to herself.

'What makes you think my brother knows where your sister is?'

It was her turn to raise an eyebrow. She hoped it would raise his hackles. 'Clearly you've been working too hard. I've been told you're a man with his finger on the pulse.' She made a little moue. 'But maybe I've been misinformed.'

Those dark eyes narrowed. 'What game are you playing now, I wonder, MJ?'

He didn't look the least enraged, not even a little put out. It occurred to her then that she didn't actually want to see him angry, but she did want to fire him to action. 'It appears our siblings have been secretly dating for…well…at least two months, though I suspect it's been longer.'

His nostrils flared. 'What proof do you have?'

Sucking her bottom lip into her mouth, she gnawed on it for a moment before releasing it. He stared at her mouth, and in the depths of his eyes something flared—something warm, inviting and terribly intriguing. But then he raised a mocking eyebrow and it startled a laugh from her. Did he think she was trying to disconcert him with her wiles and *seduce* him?

If she'd had the time, she'd have thrown her head back and laughed until fat tears rolled down her face. Bad, bad move. Nobody liked being laughed at.

Focus. How much should she tell him? If she wanted to find Siena, she was going to have to take a risk or two. And she'd risk everything for her twin.

Uncrossing her legs, she planted her feet firmly on the floor and folded her hands in her lap. 'Two weeks ago Siena and my father had a huge row. And when I say huge, I mean a row of truly monumental proportions. Ugly things were said on both sides.'

Things that could never be unsaid. The kind of things that not even MJ, in her role as family mediator, was sure she'd ever be able to help smooth over. She understood them both so very well— understood why they didn't get each other—and loved them with all her heart. If only they'd stop being so stubborn!

'And in the heat of the moment she told your father that she's dating Christian to get a rise out of him, because she knows it's the one thing he'd most hate to hear.'

That surprised a laugh from her. 'If she really wanted to outrage him, she'd have said she was dating you. You are, after all, CEO of the Leto Group, not your brother.'

The Constantinoses and the Mabels owned rival five-star hotel chains. The Mabel Group of hotels was known for its old-world charm and understated elegance, while the Leto Group's was pure glamour and over-the-top glitz.

Dark eyebrows rose and the bump on the bridge of his nose grew more pronounced. She wondered how he'd broken it. She'd love to ask and…

Stop it!

Focus. She needed to find Siena. 'So…ugly fight,' she repeated. 'I tried to smooth things over, which of course backfired. What's the saying— no good deed goes unpunished? Anyway, the upshot of all that is Siena is now no longer talking to me.'

'And why should I care about your petty family dramas, Ms Mabel?'

'Heavens! We've gone from Marjorie to MJ to Ms Mabel. What's next? Madam?'

She could've sworn his lips twitched.

'No, that's all just background context for you.' She wrinkled her nose. 'I'm not especially proud of what I did next. Long story short, I pretended to be Siena and met with a couple of her girlfriends.'

She'd dropped into the bar they frequented

most Thursday nights. 'They wanted to know how come I hadn't left with Christian yet, how romantic it all was, how handsome he is—though I won't sport with your patience by giving a blow-by-blow account of your brother's physical virtues. And they also wanted to know if she'd confided in me yet, her nearest and dearest twin.'

He leaned towards her. 'Are you telling me they couldn't tell the difference between you and Siena?'

She spread out her hands. '*That's* what you want to take away from what I just told you?' Rather than the fact that it sounded as if Siena and Christian had eloped. He raised an eyebrow and she shrugged. 'People see what they expect to see…what they want to see.'

'Which means you maybe saw what you wanted to see too. It's possible Siena's girlfriends played you.'

'I've had twenty-seven years to study my sister, Nikos. My impersonation of her is pretty damn good.' Better than Siena's was of MJ. 'You also need to understand that Siena's friends are arty types, not…'

'Not cut-throat businesswomen used to dealing with subterfuge and deceit.'

Was that what he thought she was—a cut-throat businesswoman? She shook the thought away. 'Once I heard Siena's and Christian's names linked, I visited my godmother, Lady Charlotte Hamilton.'

His lip curled. 'Tottie Hamilton is the biggest gossip in London.'

'She certainly keeps her ear to the ground. And she doesn't tell half of what she knows either, which makes the mind boggle. But she confirmed Siena and Christian *have* secretly been seeing each other for the last two months.'

'And you now want my help to bring an end to their relationship.'

She should've realised that was what he'd think. And what he'd want to do. 'No.' She said the word as gently as she could. 'Siena is twenty-seven years old, and Christian is what…twenty-eight? They're adults. I'm not going to tell my sister who she can and can't date.'

'Let me be clear, Marjorie. I won't allow a union to occur between our families. Do I make myself understood?'

'Excellent!' She beamed at him. 'We're back on a first-name basis. It's so much friendlier, don't you think?'

'Do you hear me, *Marjorie*?'

He made it sound as unfriendly as he could and it was all she could do not to roll her eyes. His vehemence and the darkness that gathered on his brow had her stomach clenching, though. 'The sentiment doesn't surprise me.' After all, it was a sentiment her father shared. 'Though I confess I'd hoped for better from you.'

His eyes narrowed. He looked as soft as granite. 'I wonder, then, what it is you *do* want from me.'

'I've already told you. I want to find Siena. I've searched in all of her usual haunts, as well as the unusual ones. She's nowhere to be found. Which means she's with Christian.'

'And you think I can find them?'

'Yes.' She put on her bravest front. 'And I want you to take me along with you when you do it.'

His jaw slackened and so did his spine. Only fractionally. *Finally*, she'd surprised him. She only noticed because she'd become so adept at reading people since she'd started working at the Mabel Group. *Not* because she was a cut-throat businesswoman.

He folded his arms. 'No.'

'I've reason to be concerned about my sister's health.'

Neither Siena nor their father would easily forgive her if she divulged the nature of Siena's illness. It wasn't her place to discuss Siena's health with anyone. Her twin guarded her privacy jealously. Normally MJ wouldn't have mentioned as much as she already had. But…

One shouldn't take chances with polycystic kidney disease! If only Siena would return MJ's calls.

She pulled in a breath; let it out again. There

was still time. As soon as she spoke to Siena, she'd know where her sister's head was at. She'd know what she needed to do and how to fix everything.

'No,' Nikos repeated.

She inched forward and rested her arms on his desk. 'Even if I tell you I'm talking about a possible life-and-death issue?' She locked eyes with him. 'Do you really hate us that much?'

CHAPTER TWO

MJ'S WORDS SENT ice surging through Nikos's veins. He had to fight competing impulses. The first was to remain in his seat with a carefully bland expression on his face like a civilised man. The other was to grab her by the upper arm, physically frogmarch her to his front door and toss her onto the street as if he were a bouncer. Or a hoodlum.

Damn it. He was a civilised man, and he had no intention of allowing a member of the Mabel family to provoke him into doing something he'd regret.

Do you really hate us that much?

The short answer was *yes*!

It was an ugly confession to make, even silently to himself, but the Mabels had brought nothing but misery and wretchedness to the Constantinos family. When Joan Mabel had tricked his grandfather into believing she loved him, her perfidy had sent the older man into a spiral of self-hatred that had resulted in him exiling himself from the world and becoming a hermit.

And when MJ's father, Graham Mabel, had seduced Nikos's mother... Nikos's hands clenched. It had destroyed his parents' marriage. He'd witnessed the fallout from that with his own eyes—

the anger, the anguish, the despair. The ugliness. It had been a blight on his childhood.

While he might not be able to hate MJ personally—he didn't know her well enough, thank God—he could still hate the idea of her. He could hate the harm her family had inflicted on his. He could hate all the Mabels had taken from him and his. He could hate that she'd profited at his family's expense.

So, yes, he supposed he did hate her that much.

'Your silence speaks volumes, Nikos.'

Good.

But, when he glanced into her eyes, it wasn't hatred that filled his veins. Her eyes looked so deep, honest and true. All a lie, of course, but right now he found that hard to remember.

'Such a progressive attitude,' she teased. 'I can see there's no thoughts of burying the hatchet in your world view.'

There was real amusement in her voice beneath the deeper thread of worry for her sister. He wanted to respond to it but he'd be a fool if he did. She was only toying with him, as her father had with Nikos's mother and her great-aunt had with his grandfather. He wasn't falling into that trap.

He shouldn't need reminding how dangerous MJ was. There'd been that incident in a nightclub eight years ago. He'd been twenty-four—old enough to know better. She'd only been nineteen, and already a siren. If he was being honest, he'd been far too aware of her that evening, had found it difficult to drag his gaze away from her.

Which had proved lucky for her. She'd been making her way to the dance floor when a drunken lout had lurched into a waitress carrying a tray full of drinks. Before he'd realised what he was about, Nikos had leapt to his feet and yanked MJ out of harm's way before five cocktails in fragile glasses, a tray and a drunken lout could crash into her. Instead the glasses had shattered to the floor around them and the tray had rolled away, while the drunk had regained his balance and kept weaving through the room.

'Oh, wow. Thank you, I…'

And then her gaze had collided with his and her words had stuttered to a halt, but the impact of her gaze had nearly felled him. She'd half-lain in his arms, her eyes huge and the beginnings of a smile trembling on her lips, and he'd been held spellbound.

Some measure of common sense had eventually kicked in. He'd forced himself to right her and set her back on her feet. She'd smoothed a hand down her orange silk blouse and had shaken out her hair, which looked softer and shinier than the silk of her shirt. 'Thank you, that could've been nasty.'

'A pleasure.' Their gazes had caught and clung and in that moment he'd felt that he knew her, deep down in his bones, in a way that made no sense. The air had shimmered as if electrically charged.

Music had started to throb around them and she'd drawn in a ragged breath and gestured towards the dance floor with an unsteady hand, her gaze not leaving his for a moment. 'Would you like to…?'

He'd nodded, not wanting the moment to end, knowing he was being offered something precious. But before he'd been able to take a single step, his date's scarlet-tipped fingers had wrapped around his upper arm and she'd pulled him back from the brink.

'I don't think so,' Cynthia had said. 'Back off, MJ.'

MJ had blinked and then lifted her hands in the universal sign of non-aggression, thanked him again, before turning and walking away. He'd watched her go, feeling he'd missed out on something momentous. He still woke in the middle of the night sometimes, remembering it.

That proved exactly how dangerous MJ could be. He'd known who she was that night and yet he'd still been prepared to follow her onto that damn dance floor, and probably anywhere else she'd wanted to lead him.

Idiot! He would *not* repeat the mistakes of past. He refused to inflict that kind of pain on his father and grandfather.

As for her worry for her sister… He hardened

the places inside him that were in danger of softening. It wasn't his problem. No matter how much he told himself that, though, he couldn't make himself feel it.

She leaned towards him, all amusement gone. 'Doesn't it exhaust you, carrying around all of this animosity?' Her brow creased. 'Do you really mean to pass that burden onto your children?'

He stiffened. He would *not* allow the Mabels to harm so much as a single hair on the head of any children he might be lucky enough to father one day.

'Maybe a match between Siena and Christian would be a good thing,' she mused. 'Maybe it would help heal old hurts.'

He stabbed a finger on his desk. 'Over my dead body!'

She stared at it then grinned. 'You've no idea how tempted I am to turn this conversation into a gangster movie and say, *That can be arranged.* Except I'm afraid you might actually believe me.'

Her grin was a lopsided affair that had mischief dancing in her irrepressible eyes the colour of laurel leaves—too dark for emeralds but not dark enough for a pine forest. His heart gave a giant kick. They promised shade. And rest. And relaxation.

Damn it! Who cared what colour her eyes were? Besides, her mouth was too wide. A fact that grin only highlighted.

Ha! He might want to find that a flaw, but it was only a flaw in the same way Julia Roberts' mouth was flawed. Which meant it was gorgeous and almost impossible to resist.

Therein lay the fatal flaw. Apparently certain members of the Constantinos clan found certain members of the Mabel family temptation personified, and it was startling to discover he wasn't exempt from their number. Despite all he knew about them. Despite the destruction he'd witnessed them wreak on people he loved.

Except he was made of sterner stuff. His hands clenched. He *would* resist. He'd resisted eight years ago. And he'd resist again now.

She glanced at his hands and the fists they formed. Her shoulders and chest lifted as she dragged in a breath and then dropped as she released it. Not a sigh, but something deeper and more heartfelt.

She's toying with you.

He hardened his heart.

She eased back and crossed her legs. 'Very well, I'll speak to you in a language you'll respond to, rather than attempt to appeal to your better nature. I know you must have one buried deep down, but I can see you're not going to dust it off for me. So, Mr Constantinos...'

He ground his teeth together, forcing himself to focus on her words rather than the lips uttering them.

'Consider, if you will, the headlines that would appear in the papers if Siena were to fall seriously ill—or worse—in the company of your brother.'

It took a moment for her words to sink in. When they did, he found himself on his feet, everything clenched so hard he'd started to shake.

'Don't look at me like that. It's something I'd like to avoid as well.'

He strode to the window. It looked out on the quiet elegance of the square, but none of the square's peace or orderliness could work its magic on him at the moment. The feud between the Constantinoses and the Mabels was well known—notorious, even. If Siena were to fall ill while with Christian, there'd be allegations of foul play—as if Christian had somehow orchestrated her illness as some form of dastardly revenge.

His brother couldn't have found his way out of a wet paper bag, let alone plan such a thing, but that wouldn't stop the rumours, the innuendos. Graham Mabel and his daughters would milk it for all they could too, no doubt. His family had suffered enough. He would *not* allow his kind, hapless brother to become the latest in a line of victims. He wouldn't allow the rocky relationship between his father and brother to disintegrate even further.

He swung round from the window.

'And yet he continues to look at me as if I

planned this whole thing,' she said to the bust on his filing cabinet.

'It wouldn't surprise me to discover you had!' He regretted the words the moment they left his mouth. They were too unbridled, too childish.

'Wow.' Her whispered word seemed to fill the room right to its very corners. Not a trace of amusement stretched in her eyes now or lurked at the corners of her mouth. She tilted her chin, everything about her hard and determined. 'If I refuse to let my father's hate control me, you can rest assured I won't let yours either, Nikos.'

He blinked. He almost believed her.

'So,' she said when he remained silent. 'Are you going to help me find them?'

'You can rest assured that I'll find them, MJ. You needn't doubt that for a moment.'

'So far, so good.'

'But you won't be accompanying me on my search, tagging along like a—'

He broke off. He was a civilised man. He refused to descend to insults.

Those damned eyes danced again, reminding him of a shady inlet on his grandfather's Greek island, the sea dancing in the sun as a breeze ruffled its surface. 'Were you going to say, like a piece of unwanted baggage…or a bad smell… a thorn in your side, perhaps?

Whatever she saw in his face had her throwing back her head and laughing. He shifted. He didn't understand this woman at all.

She swiped her fingers beneath her eyes, her merriment slowly fading. 'That, however, is not such excellent news.' She cocked her head to one side. 'I could be an asset, you know.'

He seriously doubted that.

'I know my sister better than anyone else on the planet. I'm hoping you know Christian just as well. Are the two of you close?'

He strode back behind his desk. 'None of your business.'

Those green eyes weighed him up. 'So that's a yes, then.'

She said the words almost to herself and he could've kicked himself for being so transparent. Except he hadn't been. He'd kept his usual armour firmly in place.

'Which means if we put our heads together we should be able to predict where they are and what they'll do. And how they'll react in any given situation.'

'If I need your input, I'll call you.' The less time he spent alone with this woman, the better. Nothing she could say would convince him to change his mind.

'So implacable,' she mused. 'And yet I still think I can convince you to let me tag along.'

'I think not.'

'Nikos, if you personally help me find my

sister—and that includes allowing me to tag along as a piece of unwanted luggage—then you have my word that I will give you the Ananke necklace.'

His heart kicked so hard against the walls of his chest that for a moment he couldn't breathe. Had she just said...? 'You lie.' The words scraped out of him, leaving his throat raw. 'It's not yours to give.'

Those green eyes didn't falter. 'My great-aunt gave it to me on my twenty-fifth birthday.'

He slashed a hand through the air 'The word of a Mabel is worthless.'

But...*the Ananke necklace*. The heirloom his grandfather had given to Joan Mabel fifty years ago when they'd embarked on their whirlwind affair—when he'd asked her to marry him and she'd said yes. The heirloom she'd refused to return when she'd betrayed his grandfather with another man.

The Ananke necklace belonged to *his* family.

'You might not trust me, but do you trust Bayard Crawford?'

He glanced up at the name of the prominent London lawyer. Not her family's lawyer, nor his family's lawyer either. The man had an impeccable reputation.

'I had him draw up a contract.'

If he could win the necklace back for his grandfather before the old man died...

She reached into her handbag, drew out several folded sheets of paper and handed them to him.

'As you'll see from his attached note, the necklace is currently in his keeping. So you can drop any of your nasty suspicions that I'll simply make the necklace disappear.'

Her words made him feel petty. No doubt a result of one of the many tactics she had in her arsenal. She remained silent as he read over the contract. It was above board and water-tight, though there were provisions protecting her from him giving her the slip, abandoning her or otherwise misleading her.

His lips twisted. Whose suspicions were petty now? He was a man of honour. When he entered into a contract, gave his word...

He stilled. A Mabel would no sooner believe a Constantinos than a Constantinos would a Mabel. She no more trusted him than he did her. He glanced at her. Over the years he'd demonised her family—he knew that. But maybe she *was* a woman of her word.

It didn't change the fact that he'd love to cut her dead. Every instinct he had warned him against spending any time alone with her. But the image of the Ananke necklace dangled before him, a provocative prize. If he could win it back, nearly any price would be worth that. Even being forced to spend time in the company of a Mabel.

His gut clenched. But she needed to learn that *he*

was boss. The sooner she understood that, the better. In two strides he was in front of her, his hands slamming down to grip the arms of her chair, locking her in as he drew his face close to hers. 'Why would you give me the Ananke necklace?'

'I'm not *giving* it to you. I'm *buying* your co-operation. I want to find my sister.' Her eyes flashed and she lifted her chin. It angled her lips towards him in a way that had his heart thudding too hard against his ribs, but he sensed she was entirely unconscious of that fact.

'The necklace is a curse, Nikos. It's brought far more pain than joy. I don't want it. I never wanted it.'

He didn't believe that for a moment. 'Then why haven't you got rid of it?'

She hesitated. 'My intention was to donate it to a museum.'

Did she expect him to believe that? 'And now you mean to give it to me?'

'As long as you keep your side of the bargain.'

'Your father will never forgive you.'

That determined chin lifted a notch. 'Yes, he will. I'll make sure of it.'

'How?'

She eased her spine from the back of her chair and leaned in close, so close their breaths mingled. He called himself every kind of fool for having played this game in the first place, for drawing near in an attempt to intimidate her. She didn't look alarmed or cowed, merely intrigued. And now he was in a hell of his own making because, if he wanted to maintain face, he had to remain exactly where he was. That was what he got from trying to be tyrannical. And it served him damn well right.

'Love.' She said the word clearly.

He wanted to scoff, but his throat had drawn tight and an ache started up at the centre of him.

'I love him and he loves me. He'll be in a temper—there's no doubt about that. He might not understand why I've done it, but he'll forgive me in the end. Because he knows in his heart how much I love him.'

She moistened her lips and he couldn't help but follow the action. She had pretty lips—not too full and not too thin; they looked soft and firm in exactly the right proportions. When he glanced into her eyes again, they'd widened, and he could read the surprise in their depths. Had she recognised the desire burning at the back of his own eyes?

His hands clenched so hard on the arms of her chair, his fingers started to ache. He wanted her to be as apprehensive as he was. 'Do you really want to spend that much time alone with me?'

'Needs must,' she whispered.

Her sudden breathlessness told him she wasn't as unaffected as she'd like to appear. The spectre of her in his arms eight years ago rose in his mind. His heart pumped too hard and fast. The ache that had flooded him then burst back to life now. 'What would you do if I kissed you?'

Very gently she placed a hand in the middle of his chest and pushed him back, rising to her feet, ensuring there was at least three feet between them before she drew her hand back to her side. 'Why, I'd slap you, of course. It's what all the best heroines do in those old classic movies.'

She spoke lightly as she moved to the window and he couldn't contain a rueful smile. The woman had class—he had to give her that.

She turned back to face him. 'My sister is worth a hundred Ananke necklaces. So, Nikos, do we have a deal?'

'Yes.'

'Excellent.' She pulled in a breath. 'I'd like to get started on the search as soon as possible. While you haven't bothered to enquire after my sister's health, she could be dangerously ill. Time *is* of the essence.'

Shame hit him then. Shame and guilt. Siena might be a Mabel, but she was also a human being. Where the hell was his common decency?

Where the Mabels were concerned, he had a feeling he had none. For the first time, he wondered what the hell he was in danger of turning into.

He dragged in a breath. 'Then let's not waste time. Let's get started immediately.'

CHAPTER THREE

MJ REMAINED SILENT as Nikos punched a number into his phone. 'Christian, it's Nikos. Give me a call as soon as you get this. Something has...' he glanced at MJ '...come up.'

He slipped his phone into his top pocket and it drew her attention to the breadth of those shoulders and the hard height of him.

'Right. It'll be quicker to take a cab than to drive.'

She started, had to shake off the strange lethargy threatening to steal over her. *Focus*. She'd wanted to fire Nikos to action and, now that she had, she needed to rise to the challenge.

Hooking her handbag over one shoulder, she worked at making her face politely bland. 'I guess that depends on where we're going.'

'Christian's flat.'

'In that case, it'd be quicker to take the Tube.'

He didn't answer that, just started the shutdown procedure on his computer.

'But if we did that,' she continued, 'someone might see us together, and the sky would fall in, right?'

He threw her an irritated glare. She seemed to do that a lot—irritate him. She wasn't sure how she felt about that. Not that it mattered, of course.

All that mattered was finding Siena. Once that was done, she and Nikos could go their separate ways.

Unless Siena and Christian had fallen in love and were planning to marry. In which case she and Nikos would be thrown together at family events. Hmm...could she imagine Christmas dinner, all of them one big happy family?

'What's so amusing now?'

She shook her head. 'As you won't find it the least bit funny, I'll spare you the details.'

'No, no,' he said with chilling courtesy. 'By all means share the joke.'

She lifted her chin. He'd asked for it. 'I was imagining all of the family Christmases that would feature in our future if Siena and Christian marry.'

His mouth dropped open, and then his brow grew progressively darker as he came from behind his desk. 'Why didn't you put a stop to their relationship?'

She took the two steps that brought them toe to toe and she squared off. 'You want me to forbid my younger sister by forty minutes from dating someone? Seriously? Has that approach ever worked for you in the past with Christian?'

He stared back, an arrested expression on his face, and then he wheeled away.

They caught a black cab to Christian's flat. When they arrived, she was tempted to say she'd wait for him in the car. She already knew this was a wasted journey.

She made sure to remain hidden behind him when he rang the doorbell.

'Señor Constantinos.' Luisa, the Spanish house-keeper, greeted him. 'Señor Christian is not in.'

'Do you know what time he'll return?'

'I'm afraid not.' She caught sight of MJ. 'Se-ñorita Mabel. He has not returned since you were here last.'

MJ sensed Nikos stiffen. 'I didn't think he would've, but we thought it best to check.' She hesitated. 'How long has he been gone?'

The older woman glanced at Nikos, who gave her a nod.

'Ten days.'

Ten days! They'd been gone longer than she'd thought. It took a super-human effort not to reach out and wrap her fingers around Luisa's arms. 'Did you see my sister prior to that? Was she here with him?'

Again, Luisa glanced at Nikos. Again, he nod-ded. *'Si,'* she said.

MJ's heart pounded so hard it was difficult to get her words out. 'Can you tell me how she looked? How she seemed? I understand it's only an impression,' she added quickly when the other woman started to turn away, 'but Siena has been unwell and I'm worried about her. It's why I need to find her. I want to make sure she doesn't become any sicker.'

Nikos shifted his weight to the balls of his feet. 'We'd appreciate any information you can give us, Luisa. I'm concerned that Christian might be unaware of Siena's condition.'

'*Si*. Yes. I have seen her,' Luisa finally said on a sigh. 'She stayed here for several days.'

MJ could feel Nikos tensing and bristling, but he didn't say anything.

'How did she look?'

'She…was pale. It was clear that when she first arrived she'd been crying.'

MJ's heart clenched. Crying? Pale? Dear God, please let her sister be okay.

'Señor Christian, though, cheered her up and made her laugh.'

She managed to find a smile at that, though the shoulders of the man beside her became even more rigid, if that were possible. Rubbing a hand across her chest, she said, 'Thank you.'

'The two of them, they are good friends,' Luisa added. It sounded like a warning.

'If Siena was here for several days…' MJ bit her lip. 'Did you happen to overhear any snippets of conversation that might—?'

'Absolutely not!' The housekeeper drew herself up to her full height with a glare.

She knew asking had been a risk. She gave a wan smile. 'You can't blame a girl for trying.'

'Luisa, can you tell me where I might find my brother? Where he has gone?'

'No.'

'But—'

'It is Señor Christian who pays my wages. Not you and not his father. I'm sorry, sir, but I cannot help you any further.'

MJ stepped in before Nikos could explode. 'I'm glad Christian has such loyal staff. It speaks well of him. Thank you for talking to us, Luisa. I really appreciate it.'

Luisa surprised her by reaching out and squeezing MJ's hand. 'He's a good man, *señorita*.'

She met Luisa's gaze and nodded. 'I believe you. My sister is a great judge of character.'

'I do not think you need to worry about her so much.'

That was impossible under the circumstances, but MJ found a smile for the other woman anyway.

They returned to the waiting cab. 'Why didn't you tell me you'd already been here?'

Everything about him seemed hard and unyielding. 'Because you wouldn't have believed anything I reported to you. I figured it'd be quicker and would save an argument if you checked for yourself. Besides, it's been a few days since I dropped round, and things might've changed. I also thought Luisa might tell you more than she did me.'

He sat back with a huff.

She stared out of the window, biting the side of her thumb. Pale and crying… Over ten days ago… That would've been just after the row with their father. Just after MJ had tried to patch things up between the two of them.

'If Siena is with Christian, MJ, he will look after her—take good care of her.'

The assurance was uncharacteristic, the attempt at reassurance kind, but…

'I've no doubt your brother is a good man.'

His eyes weren't black, as she'd originally thought, but a dark brown that reminded her of the finest Swiss chocolate.

'Why, I wonder?' He spoke softly. 'Given all the history between our families, why would you think well of Christian?'

'Luisa's loyalty is a fine reference, and I trust Siena's judgement.'

'Just not her judgement in relation to her health.'

She ignored that. 'Why shouldn't I have a good opinion of Christian? Or of you, for that matter? Neither of you have done anything to injure my sister or me. This ridiculous feud between my great-aunt and your grandfather is…well… *ridiculous*. Why should it impact us? My great-aunt is dead now, and I'm of the opinion the feud should've died with her. My father and your father should never have got involved, and I don't see why we—you, me, Christian and Siena—have to buy into it either.'

Those dark eyes narrowed and his jaw firmed. 'You can't be serious.'

'Why not?' Why was he so intent on keeping the feud alive and perpetuating the enmity between their families?

A frown lowered over his face. 'You can't be serious,' he repeated. 'You don't…?'

'What?'

Before he could answer, the cab pulled to a halt outside an exclusive London club. MJ had been here too.

'Want me to wait, sir?'

'No, thank you.' He paid the driver and then turned back to MJ. 'This is Christian's club.'

She blew out a breath. 'Far be it from me to point out the obvious, but it's only just gone midday. It's not exactly what I'd call club hours.

He waved that away. 'Christian often lunches here. He sometimes even works from here.'

That sounded like something her research should've uncovered.

Unlike his brother, Christian hadn't gone into the family's hotel business. Instead he was making a name for himself as an up-and-coming fashion designer. It was one of the things he and Siena had in common, MJ supposed—their creativity. Rather than being a clothing designer, though, Siena was a mixed-media artist. She'd had a couple of small exhibitions and had won a couple of commissions. Her sister was wonderfully talented and MJ didn't doubt that she'd make her mark in the art world.

The interior of the club was pure tradition, and as far from *avant garde* as one could get with its wood-panelled walls, high ceilings and lush Axminster carpet. MJ made her way to the bar and hiked herself up onto a stool. 'Hi, Big Dave.'

The bartender nodded. 'What can I get you, MJ?'

'The usual.'

He glanced at Nikos. 'Sir?'

'I'll have what she's having.' Nikos settled on the stool beside her. 'So you've been here too?'

'I'm a cut-throat businesswoman, remember? I do my due diligence.'

His lips twisted. 'Naturally.'

Had he honestly thought he'd been her first port of call? Fat chance. He was her plan of last resort. 'This is Christian's brother, Nikos,' she said when Big Dave placed their drinks in front of them.

Big Dave rested his forearms on the bar. 'I haven't seen your sister.' He shifted his gaze to Nikos. 'Or your brother in here for over a week. I checked with the other lads and none of them have either.'

She nodded. It was what she'd been expecting. 'Thanks, Big Dave.'

Nikos sipped his drink, then shot her a surprised look. 'Lime and soda?'

'It's a little early in the day for me to be drinking anything heavier.' She didn't tell him she was a teetotaller, and therefore it was always too early in the day as far as she was concerned. He'd probably take it as a sign of weakness. 'What were you expecting?'

'I had no idea.'

She found herself suddenly grinning. 'For the first time ever, I wish my usual was *crème de menthe*.'

His lips actually kinked upwards. It felt like a win.

'Big Dave.' He called the bartender back over. 'Are Raymond Diaz, Freddy Smythe or Solomon Golding here by any chance?'

The bartender nodded. 'If you don't find them in the reading room, then try the billiards room.'

'I'll wait for you here,' MJ said. 'I suspect you'll have more luck without me in tow.'

Across the bar, Big Dave gave a chuckle and Nikos raised his eyebrows.

She wrinkled her nose. 'My last meeting with them didn't go so well.'

Nikos returned fifteen minutes later. 'Any joy?' she asked.

He thumped down onto the stool beside her. 'None.'

He pulled out his phone and dialled a number— Christian's again, she suspected. This time when it went to voicemail, he didn't leave a message.

Instead he ended the call with a savage punch of his finger.

'At least you didn't yell at them,' she offered. 'Apparently I could be heard all the way in here.'

'You yelled at them?'

'They were being *seriously* irritating. All fake ignorance and holier-than-thou platitudes—but beneath it all ran a whole swathe of "I know more than you do, but I'm not going to tell you" superiority that really got up my nose.' She shrugged. 'And I was tired.' She'd barely slept for three days.

Big Dave laughed. 'Which is why you tipped your drink into Freddy's lap?'

'*He* was being the most irritating. He's never forgiven me for turning down a drunken pass he made at the Davenells' silver wedding anniversary party.'

'You tipped your drink in his lap?' Nikos asked. She couldn't work out if that was surprise or admiration in his voice.

'And then I was asked to leave and escorted to the door.'

Nikos swung back to Big Dave. 'You kicked the lady out?'

Big Dave raised his hands at the dangerous edge in Nikos's voice. 'Not me. I wasn't on that day. I heard about it second hand. I'd never ask MJ to leave.' He stroked his jaw. 'I'd be tempted to give Freddy Smythe a clip around the ear, though.'

'You and me both,' Nikos muttered, draining his drink and setting the glass on the bar before turning back to MJ. 'Ready to go?'

She slid off her stool with a wave in Big Dave's direction and followed him to the door. 'Where to now?'

'Devon.'

Devon?

'Something Diaz let slip informed me my brother is no longer in the city. Freddy kicked him before he could reveal any more, and he recovered beautifully…and they thought they'd got away with it.'

But he was a cut-throat businessman who could smell weakness at fifty paces. It would never do to underestimate this man. 'So we're going to your family estate in Devon.'

He hailed her a cab and gave the driver her address before handing her into the car. 'I'll collect you in an hour. It might be wise to pack for a couple of days.'

She nodded and then met his gaze. 'I'll pack my passport too. Just in case.'

He hesitated and then nodded before closing the cab door behind her.

Nikos pulled the car to halt in front of the Georgian manor house his maternal grandfather had gifted to his daughter as a wedding present, and glanced across at the sleeping woman beside him.

With her face in repose, the pallor of MJ's skin and the dark circles under her eyes that the force of her personality and ever-present humour had masked were now evident. As he stared at her, something in his chest shifted. MJ's worry for her sister was no longer academic, but a real and vital concern.

Ice crept across his skull. What *was* wrong with Siena? And what kind of mess had Christian landed himself in?

They were questions he hoped to find the answers to by day's end. A glance at the clock on the car's dashboard informed him there were still a few hours left. And sitting here staring at MJ wasn't going to help him find the answers.

He doubted she'd thank him for letting her sleep, and he had no intention of carrying the damn woman into the house. An armful of warm, sleepy MJ…

He cut the thought dead.

Reaching across, he went to touch her forearm, but halted. Her arm was bare…and in her lap. Too close to her legs, breasts and things he didn't want to accidentally brush if she moved. Instead he gave her shoulder a soft shake—a shoulder covered in the cotton of her slightly silly, holiday vibe T-shirt—but even the brief touch had her warmth filtering from his fingertips into his bloodstream and told him how delicate and fine were the bones there.

Her eyes opened and she blinked a few times before glancing at him. And then she smiled. The force of it punched the breath from his body.

Her smile wasn't a sultry, seductive invitation. There were no come-hither overtones. It was simply her default expression.

And it was the sexiest thing he'd ever seen.

'We're here.' The words croaked from him.

She straightened, stretched. 'What time is it?'

'Four-thirty.'

'Wow, we made good time.' She turned to the house and stilled. 'It's beautiful.' She glanced back at him. 'This is where your mother lives, isn't it? Is she nice?'

'So many questions.' His words were meant as an admonishment, but that was not the way they emerged. He shook himself. 'Of course my mother is nice. Why do you ask? Unfortunately—' or perhaps he should have said 'fortunately' '—she's not here at the moment.' His mother was currently living in New York with her second husband.

'Well, that's a shame. I've met your father and Christian, of course, but never your mother.'

She wouldn't have. His mother shunned London. She spent as much time away from England as she could. He frowned. Was MJ really ignorant about what had happened eighteen years ago? Did she really not know about the torrid affair between her father and his mother...and the painful fallout that had resulted?

She pushed out of the car as if she was looking forward to stretching her legs, checking her phone as she did so. 'Has Christian called you back?'

He swung away to collect their bags from the boot, his gut clenching. 'Not yet.'

'*Nada* from me too.' She sighed.

The familiar sounds of Rufus's and Seth's barking greeted him as the dogs raced from the house, and he knew Mrs Digby would be waiting for them on the threshold with the door wide open. He smiled in anticipation of the hot drink and shortbread or cake that would be imminent.

'Were you expecting otherwise?' It was clear to him that Siena had gone into radio silence.

He didn't know what alerted him that something was wrong. Maybe the fact MJ hadn't answered him. Or perhaps it was the unnatural stillness that seemed to emanate from her and descended around him, even though he couldn't see her, as she was currently obscured by the raised boot of the car.

He stepped round and took one look at her face—eyes fixed on the dogs, her face bled of colour and her muscles clenched so hard she'd frozen to the spot—and he was galvanised into action.

'Sit!' he instructed the dogs before they could reach her. She couldn't know that they'd have rushed right past her in their eagerness to greet him. They skidded to a halt. MJ didn't even flinch at his shouted command.

Two steps brought him to her side. Her eyes were so wide and wild it looked as if the sky could have fallen into them. They never left the dogs. He stepped in front of her to block them from view.

'MJ?'

Nothing.

'MJ, look at me.' He lifted her chin, forcing her to meet his eyes. 'You're frightened of dogs?'

'B-b-big dogs…. T-t-terrified,' she stammered between chattering teeth. 'Attacked. Six.'

Attached when she'd been six years old, or had there been six dogs? He wanted to swear.

He ran his hands down her arms, wanting to offer her the comfort of human touch, aching to rid her of her gut-wrenching terror.

Her fingers lifted to dig into his forearms, as if to anchor herself. Words fell from her lips. 'I have a s-s-scar.' Her laugh held a hysterical edge. 'Sienna too. They…' She gulped. 'It ran so fast at us.'

It? There'd only been one dog, then. He sent up a prayer of thanks. But it had obviously hurt her. And Rufus and Seth had run at her the way it must have, forcing her to relive what looked to be her worst nightmare.

'Oh, lass, they won't hurt you.' Mrs Digby appeared at his side. 'This pair are lambs.'

But he knew MJ was too far gone to heed her words.

'Would you take them into the kitchen, Mrs Digby?'

Without another word, the housekeeper returned to the house with the dogs. With a smothered oath, Nikos pulled MJ against his chest, running his hands up and down her back to warm her up, but she simply stood there frozen as if lost in her nightmare memory. Beneath his hands she felt so small and frail. He lifted her into his arms and strode into the house, through to the drawing room. Setting her on the sofa, he poured a brandy and then sat beside her and forced a mouthful of the amber liquid between her lips.

The moment it hit the back of her throat, she coughed. And coughed and coughed. Colour flooded her face. 'What are you trying to do? Kill me?' She pushed his hand away. 'That stuff is ghastly!'

He feigned indignation. 'This is my finest brandy.'

'Then *you* drink it.'

He brought the glass to her lips again, dodging her hand when she tried to push it away again. 'One more sip.'

'No, thank you. What I need is tea—sweet, hot tea.'

'Mrs Digby will be on it.'

'Tea fixes everything.'

'One more sip, MJ. I'm going to insist. You've

had a nasty shock. This will help put the fire back in you.'

'I have plenty of fire, thank you very much.' She glared, but he refused to back down. Grumbling, she took the tumbler and had another sip, grimacing as it went down, then thrust it back into his hands. 'I'm fine now. Stop fussing.'

She obviously wasn't a fan of brandy. He downed the rest in a single swallow, finding he needed fortifying too.

And then he moved to the sofa opposite, because MJ smelled like apples and vanilla, and he was starting to feel hungry. Ravenous, actually. Now that she'd started to recover from her scare, the memory of her in his arms tugged at the edges of his consciousness. He did what he could to banish it.

Mrs Digby arrived, bearing a tea tray with a pot of tea, two cups and a sponge cake.

'Oh, that looks wonderful,' MJ said. 'Thank you so much, Mrs Digby.' Pressing her hands together, she glanced at them both, her nose wrinkling. 'I'd like to apologise. We're in the country. I should've expected dogs, but…'

But her mind had been on other things.

'I had a bad experience when I was a child. And I have a checklist of things to go through whenever I see a large dog—focus on my breathing, isolate five separate sounds, things like that. But because I was off with the fairies…'

She meant because she'd been worrying about her sister and his brother.

'Well, I just looked up, and they weren't on leads, and they were running towards me, and I'm ashamed to say I froze.'

'You'd just woken up,' he said, his voice gruff, wanting to ease the distress and embarrassment he sensed simmering beneath her apology. 'You weren't properly awake. It's only natural that you were taken off-guard.' He only wished he'd been aware of her fear so he'd have been able to prevent the episode from happening at all. 'You don't need to apologise.'

'And you don't need to worry, Miss Mabel. I'll keep the dogs in the kitchen with me.'

MJ smiled her gratitude, and the way her body sank into the sofa spoke her silent relief.

And then he realised Mrs Digby had addressed MJ by her name. Her surname, admittedly, but still… 'Is Christian here, Mrs D?'

'No, Mr Nikos. I haven't seen him in…' She cocked her head to one side. 'It'd be six weeks ago when he came with a small house party.' The older woman hesitated, glancing at MJ.

'Go on,' both he and MJ said in unison.

'Well, it was a house party that included Miss Mabel here. Though I have to say you didn't seem to take so badly to the dogs then, though I noticed at the time you kept your distance.'

MJ smiled. 'That would've been my sister,

Siena. I'm MJ—short for Marjorie Joan. And I'd much prefer it if you'd call me MJ instead of Miss Mabel.'

The housekeeper's eyes widened. 'You're the spitting image of each other.'

'Identical twins.'

Nikos frowned. It was true that MJ and Siena looked alike, but in other respects they were chalk and cheese. It amazed him that people found it difficult to tell them apart. Besides the different way they dressed, MJ moved with far more energy and purpose than Siena. Her smile was also quicker, and her answers to questions slower.

'Well, that's a surprise and there's no two ways about it. Welcome to Sedgewick House, Miss MJ. Will you be staying long, Mr Nikos?'

The housekeeper's question pulled him back. 'For the night.' He had no appetite whatsoever for a three-and-a-half-hour return journey to London this evening. And MJ looked wiped out. They'd need to put their heads together and decide where to search next. But MJ needed a decent rest first.

'Your room is ready for you.'

As it always was.

'Should I make up the Rose Room for Miss MJ or…?'

Did she think MJ and him might be an item?

'Thank you, Mrs Digby, the Rose Room sounds wonderful,' MJ said before he'd recovered his equilibrium.

Did that mean Christian and Siena had shared a room when they'd been here six weeks ago? It wasn't a question he could ask. He'd never invade his brother's privacy like that.

Seizing his phone, he sent his brother a text demanding he call ASAP. When he finished, MJ handed him a cup of tea and a slice of cake.

His stomach rumbled and she laughed. 'Sounds like you skipped lunch too.'

He should've stopped for lunch! He should've made sure MJ had some sustenance in her belly.

'Thank you for being so understanding and…' she hesitated '…kind.' She nodded, as if that was the exact word she'd been looking for. 'About the dogs and everything.'

She sipped her tea, her eyes on his face. Now that he'd seen her weariness while in unguarded sleep, he couldn't un-see it.

'I know you feel you have no reason to show any kindness or consideration to any member of my family, and you probably took no joy in having to leap to my aid like that. I'm sorry if that caused you any discomfort.'

His gut churned. The fact she was a Mabel hadn't even crossed his mind when he'd seen her frozen in terror. All he'd wanted to do was make her feel safe again.

He forced himself to eat a mouthful of cake. 'I'm not a monster, MJ.'

'Far from it,' she agreed. 'What I'm trying to

say is that I'm very grateful to you. And I'm sorry I abused your brandy,' she added, with a gravity that made him laugh. 'That's better,' she said with a smile of her own. 'You've been looking far too grave and serious, and I didn't know if it was due to my dog phobia or Christian's absence.'

That wasn't a question he wanted to answer. Instead he said, 'Tell me what happened—about the dog attack when you were small.'

She settled back against the sofa and sipped her tea. 'Siena and I were six and had gone to stay with Aunt Joan in the country for the summer. It was idyllic…until Siena and I decided to scale the wall that bordered our great-aunt's estate with her neighbour's grounds.'

She glanced at him, wrinkling her nose. 'We were young and fearless and eager to explore everything. Unbeknownst to us or Aunt Joan, her neighbours had recently acquired a guard dog to go with the expensive racehorse they'd bought. I don't rightly remember how long it took for him to find us, but it felt as if suddenly this enormous dog—and he was truly huge—started barking really loudly and running towards us. We, of course, took off as fast as our pudgy little legs would carry us.'

He grimaced. 'Except dogs run faster than people.' And they'd only been six. He bet she'd been the cutest little kid.

'Exactly.' She set down her mug. 'He caught Siena around the thigh and latched on.'

Her throat bobbed and his hands clenched.

'I didn't know what to do. There was a rake lying on the ground so I picked it up and hit him with it as hard as I could—over and over. Eventually he let go and grabbed me round the shoulder instead.'

He swore.

She blinked and straightened, seizing her tea again. 'Luckily, we'd run towards the house rather than away from it, and we were screaming loud enough to wake the dead. People came running from everywhere. The gardener reached us first and he pulled the dog off me.' She smiled. 'It was all over in the quickest of flashes.'

She paused, her eyes begging him to smile. So he smiled. 'Injuries?'

'Minor. We both had a couple of puncture marks and some bruising, and we needed a few stitches each. We were lucky.'

Yet the incident had scarred her in other ways.

She shrugged, as if it was no big deal. 'So I don't wear singlet tops and Siena doesn't wear short skirts.'

'Your scars bother you?'

She kept sipping her tea. 'No. My scars don't bother me.'

But they bothered Siena. He was starting to see that MJ would do pretty much anything for her sister—including keeping her scars hidden and giving him the Ananke necklace.

He wanted to find Siena and shake her for causing her sister so much unnecessary grief.

CHAPTER FOUR

'I'VE BEEN TO your flat and spoken to Luisa. I've been to your club and spoken to Raymond, Freddy and Solomon—and on a side note, little brother, I can't believe you're still friends with Freddy Smythe—the man's a toad. And now I'm at the house in Devon. I understand you're with Siena Mabel. Her sister is worried about Siena's health—there's a medical issue and Siena needs to see a doctor.'

He blew out a breath. 'Nobody has seen hide nor hair of you in over a week, and you're not returning my calls. If you don't ring me by morning, I'm reporting you to the police as a missing person and hiring a private detective.'

MJ winced from her seat on the sofa as Nikos ended the call with a vicious stab of his finger and threw his phone onto the coffee table, his back rigid as he paced across the room.

'It doesn't have the same effect, does it?' She nodded at his phone when he turned to pace back towards her.

'What doesn't?'

She was almost proud of him for the way he held his temper in check, careful not to direct any of it her way. 'When I was a little girl, I once saw my mother slam down the phone.' The image had stayed in her mind. She'd never seen her mother so angry. 'It was one of those old-fashioned phones with the receiver attached by a cord. You know the ones?'

He nodded.

'It looked so *satisfying* to hang up on someone by slamming the receiver down like that. Jabbing one's finger at a tiny screen is nowhere near as gratifying.'

He dropped into the sofa opposite, the storm on his brow not clearing, but his shoulders lost some of their stiffness. 'You think they've left the country, don't you? It's why you brought your passport.'

'I don't know.' She forced herself to hold his gaze, even as her cheeks heated when she recalled the sense of security that had stolen over her when she'd been in his arms, paralysed with fear.

It reminded her of that time in the nightclub eight years ago when he'd pulled her to safety. She'd simultaneously felt safer than she'd ever been and more alive than she'd ever thought possible. Something warm, sweet and laced with excitement had passed between them. She'd never wanted a man the way she'd wanted Nikos in those few short moments. The memory disturbed her.

As did this new one. The fact that, even through her terror, she'd sensed Nikos would keep her safe. It was a false impression, of course. The man hated her. Which wasn't entirely true. Nikos was beginning to realise that he only hated the idea of her. He didn't hate her personally.

She crossed her fingers in her lap.

'Marjorie?'

She shook herself. 'I can't help thinking that if they were still in the country we'd know about it. But I hope I'm wrong.'

England was a big enough area to search as it was. Once you added in the rest of the world... She closed her eyes. If she could just *talk* to Siena.

'Can you afford to take time off work like this? Last I heard, you'd been promoted to Vice President of Mabel's.'

She opened her eyes. 'I've taken a month's leave.' She was hoping it would spur her father into rethinking...things. 'As the Leto Group's CEO, can you?'

'I'll make time. Would you like a drink?'

She'd refused wine at dinner and he gestured now to the drinks cabinet. She shook her head.

'You don't mind if I...?'

'Not at all.'

He poured himself another brandy and moved back to the sofa, nursing it. A fire crackled in the fireplace. It wasn't a cold night, but the fire was cheerful, cosy, and though it was early, she found herself fighting a yawn.

'You told me Siena is angry with your father.

And you. What does she usually do when she's angry? Does she party hard in defiance? Or hide away somewhere quiet to lick her wounds?'

Her chest clenched. 'Given those two options, I'd say the former. But Siena isn't angry—not really...not any more. She's hurt.'

'What does she do when she's hurt?'

It depended on whether her hurt had turned to despair.

'Usually she'd throw herself into some project to try and take her mind off it—like her art. And talk things out...with me.' She tried to smile. 'We're sisters, so obviously we've had arguments and disagreements in the past, but they've only lasted a couple of days at most, and usually not more than a couple of hours. We've never had one that's lasted this long.'

He leaned forward to concentrate more fully on her and her words. His forearms rested on his knees, brandy balloon hanging negligently from his fingers. While the room was large, and the space between them more than generous, it felt as if the room had shrunk and that the air she was breathing was full of him.

She reached for her water, her hand shaking slightly. 'Christian adds a wild card element, and until I talk to her I can't predict what she'll do.'

'Wild card in a good or bad way?'

She needed to tread carefully. She didn't want Nikos getting his back up or jumping to unnecessary conclusions. 'I'm hoping she's turned to him the way she'd normally turn to me. From what I've heard about Christian, he's kind and sensible.'

Nikos's lips twisted. 'He's certainly kind.'

No, no, no. She wanted him to be sensible too. Siena *needed* sensible.

'He's been taken advantage of in the past.'

She wanted to swear. Really loudly. She needed Christian to see past Siena's usual tricks.

Nikos's knuckles whitened around his glass. 'What are you *not* hoping for?'

He saw too much. She bit the side of her thumb, worrying at the nail. 'I hardly know.'

Before he could call her a liar, she rushed in with a question of her own. 'Tell me a classic story about you and your brother.' It might give her a clue as to Christian's real nature and tell her how he and Siena might act—and react—together.

'What do you mean, a classic story?' He sat back and crossed his legs, seemingly at ease, but some sixth sense told her it was a pretence. 'Give me an example of one involving you and Siena and then I'll know what you mean.'

She gave a mirthless laugh. He just wanted to hold all his cards close to his chest and not share any of them. She rose. 'I think I might retire and have an early night.'

'No.' The word seemed to leave him involuntarily. 'I'm a man of my word, MJ. Quid pro quo

and all that—you give me a classic story about you and Siena and then I'll give you one about me and Christian.'

'Except you've given me nothing so far.' The way he'd handled her fear of dogs, the way he'd dealt with that situation during and after, rose through her mind now. She battled the urge to sit and tell him everything he wanted to know. 'Tell me how Christian reacts when he's in love.'

The brandy in his glass rocked wildly. 'He's not *in love* with Siena.'

Just because he wanted that to be true didn't make it so. 'I never said he was.'

His glare would have incinerated a lesser person.

'Fine, then tell me how he reacts when he's smitten…infatuated.'

He slammed his brandy on the coffee table. Leaning over, he dragged both hands back through his hair. Eventually he straightened, picked up his glass and downed what was left in it in one swallow.

He glanced up at her. She sat.

'He makes the woman the queen of his world. He'll do anything in his power to make her happy.' His gaze turned sharp, mocking. 'What does that tell you, Ms Freud?'

'He sounds like a real sweetheart.'

He leaned towards her, his eyes hard. 'But what does it *tell* you?'

'You're saying he lacks moderation,' she said slowly.

He gave a nod.

'If Siena, for example, wanted to do something reckless, would he encourage her? Or would he be the voice of reason and talk her out of doing anything silly?'

'Between those two options,' he forced out between gritted teeth, 'my money would be on the former.'

Damn, damn, damn.

'Are you telling me Siena is reckless?'

She chose her words carefully. 'Siena is an artist with an artist's temperament. In art and in life she'll sometimes seize on an idea and will follow it blindly, without thinking through where it might lead.'

Nikos nodded. 'Christian's the same.'

'Whereas I'm a thinker and planner.' She suspected Nikos was too. It was what made them so good at their jobs. 'I'm usually her voice of reason. I want Christian to be that voice of reason for her now.'

Dark eyes met hers. She reluctantly forced the words from her lips. 'From what you've told me, I'm worried Christian will become so caught up in her enthusiasm he'll follow her wherever she leads.'

'You think she'll twist him around her little finger.'

'I'll tell you two classic stories—two sides of the same coin. When Siena and I were six, we stayed in the country one entire summer. We heard rumours of an amazing apple orchard in the grounds of the castle next door. It wasn't really a castle, of course, but we pretended it was. So it follows that the apples were likewise enchanted because everything about that summer was enchanted.'

She smiled, remembering that long-ago summer. 'Neither of us had ever picked an apple straight from the tree before, and Princess Siena wanted to so very badly. But how could she get over the eight-foot stone wall that surrounded the castle?

'Well, this is where Princess MJ comes into her own. She turned her mind to the problem and worked out that, if they climbed the old oak tree on their side of the wall and walked along the wall for a way, they could then climb down a maple on the other side and be in the castle grounds.'

'You could've broken your necks!'

'Instead we found a guard dog who didn't take kindly to two little trespassers.'

He pursed his lips. 'Siena came up with the idea and you found a way to make it happen. And it ended badly.'

'Story two. When Siena and I graduated from university, Siena was obsessed with the idea of travelling to Africa. She wanted a first-hand look at African art and to practise some of the techniques for herself with a local artist. Nice idea, except her travel plans sounded haphazard at best. So I explored some options and discovered a non-denominational charity that was building schools in Africa. We decided to volunteer in Cameroon for two months. Siena didn't get to see as much art as she wanted, but the colours and impressions of the place continue to inform her work today.'

'And you, MJ? What did you get out of it beside babysitting your sister?'

'It was one of the best experiences of my life. I not only had the chance to encounter a culture vastly different from mine, but have also made lifelong friendships.'

Very slowly, he nodded. 'She had the idea, you made it happen...and it ended well.'

'Like I said—two sides of the same coin. I just don't know which way the coin will land with Christian in the picture.'

His jaw clenched.

Before he could get too caught up in angry thoughts and blame Siena for his brother's current status as a missing person, she said, 'Your turn now. You promised a classic story about Christian.'

His gaze returned to hers and his brows lowered. For a moment she thought he might make an excuse and put her off, but then he shook his head and opened his mouth. She leaned towards him...

His phone rang, the piercing ringtone making

them both jump. He jerked forward to snatch it up. 'It's Christian.'

'Put him on speaker phone,' she begged. 'I'll be as quiet as the proverbial mouse.'

After the briefest of hesitations, he nodded. It felt like another win—a sign of trust.

'Christian,' he said, answering the call. 'It's a relief to find you haven't been abducted by aliens and that I don't need to report you as a missing person.'

She resisted the urge to roll her eyes at his sarcasm.

'Very funny, Nik. Since when does it become a national crisis if I don't return your call within twenty-four hours? You better have a damn good reason—'

'Since I received a visit from MJ Mabel desperate to get hold of her sister and convinced you're the key.'

Christian remained silent.

'Is it true?' he barked.

'Actually, Nik, it's none of your damn business.'

'I'm worried about you.'

'I'm capable of looking after myself.'

'But are you capable of looking after Siena?'

'What the hell is that supposed to mean?'

For the first time, real anger entered Christian's voice and it made MJ's heart beat faster.

'You listen to me, Nik. I'm twenty-eight years

old. You need to stop sweeping in like the cavalry every time I make a decision you don't agree with. I'm not the idiot you think I am.'

Nikos blinked. 'I don't think you're an idiot.'

'I might not be the paragon you are, but I refuse to put myself in the same damn straitjacket you wear. I'm entitled to live life on my own terms. If I make a few mistakes along the way, well, I can live with that.'

Nikos massaged his temples, and MJ ached for him. Couldn't Christian see how much his brother loved him? He shouldn't be so resentful of Nikos's concern. It was obvious he'd do anything for his little brother.

Christian gave an ugly laugh. 'What you're really worried about is me tarnishing the family name and giving Father even more grief and worry. Not once has it occurred to you that he deserves the grief and worry. If he'd made different decisions…'

Nikos swore. 'You need to listen to me—'

'No!'

'MJ has offered me the Ananke necklace in exchange for me finding Siena.'

Silence greeted this announcement.

'Tell me you refused,' Christian finally said.

'Of course I didn't refuse!' Nikos exploded. 'What did you expect me to do?'

'You're just like father and grandfather!'

Nikos gripped the phone so hard his entire

body started to shake. 'And what's wrong with that?'

'You don't see it, do you?'

She had to agree with Christian there. Nikos was oblivious to how destructive this feud between the families continued to be.

'What I do know is that Siena is ill and—'

'Siena is no concern of yours.'

And then the line went dead.

Nikos turned pale. The lines bracketing his mouth deepened and his eyes flashed. He flung his phone down and paced around the room calling his brother every kind of fool. Eventually he rounded on MJ. 'What has your sister done to him?'

She shot to her feet and slammed her hands to her hips. 'Oh, right, it's all Siena's fault, is it?'

He advanced, his face twisting. 'What is wrong with her?' His nostrils flared. 'If she's on drugs…! If she gets Christian hooked on drugs, I swear I will destroy everything you love.'

MJ's eyes widened at his words. She swung to address the painting above the mantelpiece. 'And then he goes and ruins it all, just like that.'

Ruined what? Nikos ground his back molars together. There was nothing here to ruin. It was already ruined by two generations of bitterness and betrayal.

'One moment he proves he's a flesh and blood man—kind, smart, reasonable—and then...'

'And then what?' He couldn't stop from asking.

She swung round, her eyes flashing. 'And then you turn into a jerk. And a bully.'

He recoiled, but she had a point. He shouldn't have lost his temper like that. He couldn't remember the last time he'd lost it so completely. But his grandfather's stooped shoulders had risen in his mind, along with the deep lines etched into the skin around his father's mouth and the dead light in his mother's eyes. He'd do anything to prevent Christian from the kind of pain they'd suffered. Pain suffered at the hands of the Mabels.

'I'm afraid it'd keep you awfully busy, Nikos, destroying everything I love, because I love a lot of things.'

He fell onto the sofa, raking both hands back through his hair. 'Then you're a fool, MJ, because love makes you weak.'

She poured a brandy, but she didn't drink it as she walked round the room, studying the paintings on the walls. Eventually she set the brandy in front of him and left the room without another word. She didn't even bid him goodnight.

He didn't deserve a good night.

He was on his feet and in the hall before he knew it. MJ was only a quarter of the way up the stairs. 'I'm sorry I lost my temper.'

She halted but didn't look at him.

'And I'm sorry for what I said about Siena. It was unfair...out of order.'

She turned her head. 'How much did that just hurt—having to apologise to a Mabel?'

His temples throbbed. 'A lot.' But she deserved an apology.

'Good.'

The shadow of a smile touched her lips and something in his chest unhitched.

'Apology accepted. Goodnight, Nikos.'

'Goodnight, MJ. Sleep well.'

He hoped she'd have colour in her cheeks when she woke in the morning and that the dark circles beneath her eyes would have started to fade.

For the briefest moment their gazes caught and clung, and then MJ swung away and took the stairs two at a time and he forced himself back into the drawing room to drink his brandy.

The next morning Nikos found MJ hovering at the top of the stairs, peering down at the hall below. He halted and then backed up a couple of silent steps, before starting forward again with a heavier tread so as to not startle her.

She swung round, a smile in place. His gut clenched. Except her smile wasn't *in place*. It wasn't planted there as some kind of fake assurance or civility. It was real. Despite him being a bad-tempered jerk who'd tried to bully her more than once yesterday, she still sent him the kind of smile that could make the blood surge in a man's veins.

He didn't deserve her good-natured generosity. And she deserved better than his continued curmudgeonly ill humour. They'd made a deal and she'd submitted to it with grace, even though sacrificing the Ananke necklace had to be a blow. He needed to act with grace too, and not just because the necklace was a prize worth winning. He needed to prove, if only to himself, that he could be mature and reasonable in this situation.

The Constantinoses and Mabels would never be friends, but that didn't mean he and MJ couldn't behave with common courtesy and dignity. In fact, it felt imperative that they did, though if pressed he couldn't have explained why.

He dragged in a breath, suddenly aware that the silence between them had stretched for too long. 'The dogs will be locked in the kitchen.' His chest clenched. How long had she been standing up here, gathering the courage to venture downstairs? 'It's safe to go down.'

'I know I'm being silly.' She pushed a lock of hair behind her ear. 'I know they wouldn't hurt me even if I did accidentally stumble across them. It's just…'

Phobias weren't rational. She knew it and he knew it. But knowing it didn't necessarily change anything. He didn't want her feeling bad about it, so he steered the conversation to safer channels.

'Are you hungry? Ready to go rustle up some breakfast?'

'Ooh, yes please!'

Her enthusiasm made him smile. 'I take it you're a breakfast person, then?'

'I'd eat breakfast three times a day if I could.'

Her cheerful confession eased some of the tightness in his chest.

'It has all of my favourite foods—bacon and eggs, sausages, toast, porridge, croissants…even black pudding.'

She glanced up, her eyes dancing now without a trace of fear to darken their depths. He wondered where she found her good humour and optimism. She seemed to have an endless supply of both.

'What about you?' She gave a mock-groan. 'Please tell me you're not one of these paltry people who make do with a cup of black coffee as they rush out the door?'

'Not a chance. I skip lunch too often to miss breakfast. But my favourite food would be steak and potatoes.'

She rolled her eyes. 'Typical man.'

And yet she was far from a typical woman. 'And my mother's baklava.'

'Pastry, honey and nuts…' She sighed. 'Hard to beat.'

He paused outside the kitchen door. 'Wait here while I take the dogs out.'

Her hands twisted together and... Was that guilt at the back of her eyes? 'They'll be fine outside, MJ, I promise. They love to run around and play.'

'It seems hard—unfair—that they get banished because of me.'

He stared at her for a moment. 'Do you want me to leave them in?'

Fear flashed in her eyes and she shook her head, giving a funny little hiccup. 'I know I'm being a coward, but...'

'Nonsense.' He made his voice crisp. 'It's no drama and no bother.'

A few moments later he and MJ were seated at the big oak table drinking huge mugs of tea while Mrs Digby busied herself at the range, cracking eggs into a frying pan and laying rashers of bacon alongside them, the room filling with the most delicious aroma as the food sizzled and spat. Outside the windows the dogs gambolled in the garden.

'They're rescue dogs,' he said, spying her watching them. 'When Mr Digby died a few years ago, Mrs Digby thought it might be nice to have a couple of dogs here.'

Mrs Digby turned from the stove. 'It'll be four years this September that Mr D passed, God rest his soul. And with Mrs Constantinos remarrying and spending less time here, and the boys up in London more often than not...' She plated their food. 'Well, it got to being a bit lonely, like.' She set a plate in front of MJ. 'They're good company, Miss MJ. And they keep me fit.'

'And you're also giving a home to animals who need one, which is nice.'

MJ bit into a piece of toast, her eyes half-closing with bliss. It made Nikos want to laugh. She evidently hadn't been exaggerating when she said she loved breakfast.

'But why choose dogs that are *so* big?'

Her expression made them both laugh, which he suspected had been her plan.

'They're harder to place,' he said.

'And we have the room here for them to run around in.'

MJ gestured to her plate. 'This is delicious, Mrs Digby. Thank you so much.'

'There's plenty more if you want it. Just give me a yell. I'll be in the laundry room if you need me.'

Mrs Digby left and MJ's gaze returned to the window.

'Rufus was found half-dead in a ditch.'

Her knife and fork hung suspended above the food on her plate as she stared at him.

'He hadn't just been dumped. He'd been thrown from a moving vehicle. When he was found, he had a broken leg, broken ribs and multiple abrasions. For a while they weren't sure if he'd make it.'

'*What?* How could…? The poor thing! How could anyone do that to another living creature?'

He shrugged. 'Beats me. Seth's story isn't any

happier. He was found tied to a post on a short lead in a deserted yard without any shelter, half-starved and covered in sores. He's frightened of strange men. It takes them a while to earn his trust. We think a man used to beat him.'

Her cutlery clattered to her plate and her eyes filled. 'I don't believe in corporal punishment, but if I did it'd be people like that I'd...'

He nodded. 'Seth's previous owner was charged, which is something, I suppose.'

'There's no excuse for that kind of cruelty. To deliberately hurt someone or something weaker than you...' She broke off. 'It's unforgivable.'

And yet she didn't seem to view her great-aunt's behaviour towards his grandfather as either cruel or unforgivable. Though, even Nikos had to admit that, despite the fact Joan Mabel had taken advantage of his *pappoús*, the power dynamic between the couple had at least been equal.

A different kind of ice settled over him. If MJ ever found out about it, would she find what had happened between their parents unforgivable?

'Nikos?'

He shook himself. 'Sorry, what were you saying?'

'It was nothing.'

She arranged her cutlery into a neat line on her plate and pushed it away. She hadn't finished her breakfast and he wanted to thump himself. In trying to make her less afraid of his dogs, he'd robbed her of her appetite. *Way to go, Nikos.* He'd organise croissants for morning tea.

In the meantime… 'Any thoughts about where we go from here? I spent some time last night—' *when he'd been lying in bed, staring at the ceiling, strangely restless* '—trying to pinpoint where Christian might retreat to. He has friends in Paris and loves the city.'

'Siena loves Paris too—loves the art galleries.'

'We also have an apartment in Switzerland.'

'It's not ski season.' She tapped a finger against her lips. 'Which doesn't mean they haven't gone there, of course. Siena won't have retreated to any of the family's places—the villa in Spain or the apartment in Paris—because she'd worry the staff would betray her location to my father.'

She glanced at her watch. 'But the smart money is on her ringing me this morning.'

'What makes you say that?'

'She and Christian would've spent last night working out what to do—about us—and one of those things would be getting me to back off.'

Her words made sense, and no sooner had she uttered them than her phone rang. She turned it towards him so he could see the name on the screen.

Siena.

'Are you psychic?'

His words made her smile. She answered the call and put it on speaker phone. 'Thank you for calling, Siena, I've been worried sick.'

Siena sighed—a great, heaving sound that rolled down the line and made MJ wince. Nikos's hands clenched. *Seriously?* Didn't Siena have a clue what she'd been putting her sister through?

'Look, Jojo, I only have a couple of things to say and it won't take long.'

'I have a couple of things to say too. Promise me you'll hear them before hanging up on me.'

Silence followed MJ's request. If he could, he'd like to reach down the phone and shake Siena. He'd like to shake Christian too, who was no doubt sitting beside her.

'Siena?'

'Is any of it about Dad?'

'No.'

'Okay, fine.'

He doubted Siena could have been more grudging if she'd tried.

'First off, Jojo, I want you to give me some space. It doesn't seem an unreasonable request. I don't hold you responsible for anything Father said, so you can stop fretting about that. The thing is, I can't be what you want me to be either.'

'I don't want you to be anything other than happy!'

MJ's teeth worried at her bottom lip. Nikos wanted to tell her to stop it, that she'd hurt herself.

'And healthy, of course,' she added. 'That's all I want for you, Sisi.'

'It's not *all* you want. You want me to play

happy families and I can't do it. Not at the moment. Have you heard about learned dependence?'

MJ's brow wrinkled. 'What's that got to do with anything?'

'I've relied on you for too many things over the years and it's time it stopped. I want to stand on my own two feet.'

A bad taste stretched through Nikos's mouth. That refrain sounded all too familiar.

MJ briefly closed her eyes. 'When you say you want some space, how long are we talking? A week? A month?'

Siena remained silent.

'Longer?'

The panic in MJ's voice made his chest ache.

'I don't know. I'm not like you. I don't have everything plotted on a graph and every detail worked out to the nth degree.'

MJ's head rocked back.

Nikos glared at the phone. The ungrateful little witch!

'Jojo, it's not fair to use me to make you feel better and less alone because Mother's no longer here!' Siena burst out.

MJ went so white, he reached out to grip her hand.

'That's just about the meanest thing you've ever said to me,' MJ choked out.

'I don't mean it to be,' Siena said in an almost identical choked whisper, and it made MJ's eyes fill.

She gripped his hand so hard, it almost hurt. 'I haven't meant to make you feel bad, Sisi.'

Siena didn't say anything for a moment. 'If you and Nikos hire a private investigator to track us down, neither Christian nor I will forgive you. Do you hear me?'

'Loud and clear.'

There was another hesitation. 'Dad will never forgive you if you give the Ananke necklace to Nikos.'

Her chin lifted. 'Yes, he will.'

'Your faith in him is astounding. He's going to break your heart, Jojo.'

'Or maybe he'll surprise you instead. But we promised not to talk about him.' She pulled in a breath. 'Sisi, your doctor told me your test results.'

'*What?* But that's... It's an invasion of privacy!'

'To be fair, I was wearing the gypsy skirt you gave me for my birthday, so it was an understandable mistake to make.'

'And you didn't set her straight? You pretended to be me?'

'I bumped into her at our Chelsea hotel—she'd been lunching with a guest. It's not like I planned the meeting. Anyway, all she said was that she'd been trying to contact you, that you needed to come in for more tests, and she briefly mentioned why.'

Siena remained silent.

'Why haven't you returned her calls?' MJ shot

back with some of her old fire. 'You can't take
risks with your health like this and—'

'My health, my life, Jojo. I'm capable of making my own decisions on the subject.'

Nikos winced at her tone.

'But you've involved Christian. Does he know
what you've dragged him into?'

'That's what you and Nikos want, isn't it? To
break us up. Well, it's not going to happen!'

Then the line went dead, and the devastation
on MJ's face wrung his heart dry.

And then a sudden thought left him reeling—
a brutal, ugly thought.

MJ and Siena were twins. Siena had some kind
of health issue that scared the hell out of her sister.
They were twins, identical twins—identical DNA.

His mouth dried. Did that mean MJ was sick
too?

CHAPTER FIVE

MJ STRODE ACROSS to the window to stare un-seeingly out at the garden, her heart stretching thin and everything aching. She'd been so convinced that after speaking to Siena she'd know exactly where her sister's head was at, and therefore would know what to do. She'd been convinced she'd know whether Siena had real feelings for Christian or if she was using him as a kind of sticking plaster.

But she *didn't* know.

She didn't have a clue.

And it scared her senseless.

She hadn't lied when she'd told Nikos that she loved a lot of things, a lot of people. But the person she loved above all others was Siena, and if anything were to happen to her...

She closed her eyes and pressed a hand to her chest.

'Marjorie?'

She opened her eyes and forced herself to turn and meet Nikos's gaze. 'After that phone call, I'm none the wiser, Nikos. None at all, I'm afraid.'

And she *was* afraid.

He looked as if he wanted to ask something, but she didn't have the heart for any more talk. She wanted—needed—to do something. She needed action. Needed to feel in control again.

Swinging back to the window, she watched the dogs. Rufus walked around with a big stick in his mouth looking ridiculously pleased with himself, while Seth nosed a tennis ball and then went for a run, before racing back to the tennis ball. Their antics made her smile. They looked perfectly happy. And then she remembered their sad histories and straightened. Well, there was at least one less thing she could be afraid of.

Wordlessly she moved to the back door, stepped outside and closed it behind her. Both dogs stopped what they were doing to look at her, and she faltered. She was alone in the garden with two ginormous dogs. In that moment, if Nikos had opened the door behind her she'd have leapt into his arms.

Don't be a coward.

Besides, this fear of dogs, especially of this pair who were clearly far from vicious, paled in comparison to the fear that knotted her stomach whenever she thought of Siena. She forced knocking knees forward and lowered herself as steadily as she could to a stone bench.

Rufus, the braver of the two, started towards her with his stick still held in his mouth. She watched him and held her breath.

He halted and turned his head away.

Oh! 'Was I…was I eyeballing you, Rufus?' She

forced her gaze to her lap, though it felt alien to be this close to a dog and not minutely tracking its every movement. 'I'm sorry, that was rude. I don't like being stared at either.' She kept her voice low, though she couldn't always keep it steady. 'The thing is, you see, I don't really know how to act around dogs and...'

His head came into view and her words jammed into her throat. What should she do? Would he let her pat him? Did she dare?'

Very carefully he laid the stick at her feet, the gesture absolutely melted her heart. 'You're giving that to me? Oh, what a big sweetheart you are.' Reaching out, she touched his head, ran her hand down his shaggy fur to scratch his shoulder. He leaned into her touch, his bottom half-wagging in time to her scratches in an ecstasy that made her laugh. 'Well, I seem to have got the hang of making friends with you.'

In response, he laid his head in her lap and gazed up at her in undiluted adoration. 'Oh, sweetheart.' Her throat thickened and she gently tugged on his ears. 'You don't know me. I'm not sure you should be so trusting.' Now, where was Seth? Had he run away and hidden? She wouldn't blame him if he had.

She found him standing a little way to her right, watching her and Rufus. 'Hello, Seth.' She held her hand out towards him. 'Would you like a pat too?'

He started towards her, halted, took another step forward and stopped again. All the while she stroked Rufus's head in her lap and kept up a stream of what she hoped was soothing chatter. For the last few yards, Seth dropped to his tummy and almost cowered, crawling to her. Tears burned the backs of her eyes. 'Oh, Seth baby, I'm not going to hurt you. C'mon, boy.'

The moment she stroked his head, and then the tummy he promptly presented to her, he bounced up again, all excited energy. He licked her hand, her arm and her face when it got too close, making her laugh. He jumped up on the bench beside her and tried to crawl into her lap.

Not to be outdone, Rufus leapt up on the other side. She wanted to give them both big, squishy hugs. The moment felt like a gift. An unlooked-for one. Because it wasn't what she'd envisaged when she'd woken up that morning.

'Rufus, Seth—down.' The command came from behind her. Rufus jumped down immediately. 'Seth, down,' Nikos ordered again.

Seth moped to the ground with a reluctance that made her want to laugh.

'Sit.'

Both dogs sat. Nikos threw a ball and they immediately tore after it. He lowered himself to the bench beside her and she was suddenly achingly aware of the breadth of his shoulders and the power of the muscles bunched in his thighs—

all the life contained within his denim jeans and thin jumper.

A thousand butterflies filled her chest. Before this morning, she'd never seen Nikos in anything but a suit. He looked great in a suit—powerful, sexy, gorgeous.... He looked great in jeans too—approachable, sexy, gorgeous...

She tried to stamp out the feminine appreciation that welled up inside her, craning its neck for a better peek. It would do her no good. She suppressed a shudder. He'd see it as a weakness he could exploit.

He reached out and clasped her hand. 'Are you okay?'

She stared at the picture of her hand in his. 'Yes.'

'That was just about the bravest thing I've ever seen.'

She glanced up. 'That wasn't brave. Brave would be saving a child from a pack of wild dogs or—'

'Nonsense. That kind of bravery is just gut instinct—hurtling into the fray to help someone in trouble. What you did was calmly and knowingly face a fear that has crippled you for most of your life.'

He released her hand to throw the ball for the dogs again. She missed the warmth. She tried placing it in her other hand, but it wasn't the same as being held by his.

'I merely faced two dogs who I knew wouldn't hurt me—who had more reason to fear me than I them. I'd hardly consider myself cured. I'm always going to be wary around dogs I don't know.'

'That's wise. Everyone should take care around dogs they don't know.' He turned to meet her gaze. 'My heart was in my mouth when they jumped up. I'm impressed you didn't panic.'

She shrugged, trying not to let his admiration affect her. 'By then I knew it was nothing to be afraid of. Other than maybe being smothered by too much affection.'

That made him grin. He threw the ball again. 'They forget their manners when they get excited. Their education is a work in progress.'

That grin... *Oh!*

She had to look away. 'Given their histories, it must be hard not to spoil them.'

'What made you do it? What made you come out here and make friends with them?'

His voice had sobered, so she risked glancing at him. The light in his eyes didn't slow the racing of her pulse. She lifted one shoulder. 'I got tired of being afraid.'

He nodded as if her words made perfect sense. The sudden accord she felt with him shocked her.

'After that disastrous conversation with Siena, it felt like everything was starting to spin out of control.' She wrinkled her nose. 'I guess I just wanted to gain an illusion of control back again.'

88   ESCAPE WITH HER GREEK TYCOON

'Maybe I need to find something I'm afraid of so I can conquer it.' His lips twisted. 'Perhaps it'll help me get a handle on things.'

She slapped her hands to her knees. 'Well, as you're afraid of me, you needn't go far for inspiration.' The words shot out before she thought better of them.

Very slowly, he turned more fully on the bench to face her. His gaze lowered to her lips. A tic started up at the side of his jaw. 'And do you want to be conquered, Marjorie?'

The way he said her name turned her insides to molten caramel. It took an effort to wrench her gaze from his. 'Conquering me and conquering your fear of me are two very different things.'

She stood. This conversation was getting out of hand.

She swung back to him, hands on hips. 'You're implying that in sleeping with me you'd be conquering me. Why do men do that—view women as conquests?'

'Actually, I don't—'

'So often sex has to be framed as a man winning something and a woman losing or surrendering something. It's chauvinistic and damaging, and I—'

'And it's not what I truly believe, MJ.' He spoke over the top of her. 'I was just being facetious. I'm sorry.'

Heat rose in her face. 'Sorry,' she mumbled.

'It's one of my soap boxes.' She folded her arms. 'Why were you being facetious?'

'Because you hit a little too close to the bone when you said I was afraid of you.'

She wanted to cry. She made herself smile. 'I know you're not afraid of the real me, Nikos. But it doesn't stop you loathing the idea of me. The only way to overcome your antipathy is to get to know me and drop your prejudices.' But she didn't think he'd ever let that happen. He'd keep his barriers firmly in place. 'For what it's worth, that—' she gestured to the dogs '—felt like a gift.'

His lips twitched. 'You're telling me now that you're a gift?'

The thought made her smile for real. 'You bet your sweet patootie I am. It's better than being a conquest, right?'

He nodded. But he stood then, sobering. He leaned down to peer into her eyes. 'Aren't you the slightest bit afraid of me?'

His proximity made her breath stutter. She gripped her hands together so hard, they started to ache. Letting out a breath, she forced them to relax. 'I've watched you. Over the years. I mean, we move in the same circles, attend many of the same parties and business functions. I've seen the way you do business. I've even seen how you conduct yourself when a romantic relationship has ended. You work hard, you have high standards and you demand loyalty, but you don't ask for anything you can't give yourself.'

He blinked and snapped upright.

'You're ethical and you have a sense of honour. You'd never physically harm a woman, even if she is a Mabel. So no, Nikos, I'm not afraid of you. I think you're a good man.'

'You…'

He looked at a loss for words and she nodded. 'I'm worried about what you might do if you don't manage to gain a sense of perspective where our families are concerned. But as for the rest of it?' She shook her head. 'I'm not afraid of you.'

Though she was beginning to become afraid of the feelings being near him had started to engender inside her.

'Aren't you worried about giving away so much? Being so unguarded around someone who could be your enemy?'

His words confirmed what she already knew deep in her heart. He would view any attraction she felt for him as a weakness. And vice versa. If he found himself attracted to her, he'd consider it a fatal flaw.

'How do you think you can use anything I just told you against me? Besides,' she continued when he remained silent, 'I didn't say I was worried for *myself* or *my* family if you didn't gain that perspective.'

'Which only leaves me and my family.' His

eyes narrowed. 'Why would you worry for us, I wonder?'

He didn't believe her. It shouldn't surprise her. She pointed a finger, stopping short of touching his chest. 'Because I want this feud to end. And, from where I'm standing, I think you and I are our families' best hope of making that happen.'

His head rocked back. '*That's* the real reason you offered me the Ananke necklace.'

'No, that was an act of desperation. I really did want to donate it to the Victoria and Albert Museum. And, if you do help me find Siena, when I hand the necklace over to you that's what I'm going to ask you to do with it.'

He opened his mouth, as if to tell her *Over my dead body,* but she rushed on before the words could drop from his lips. 'I'm dying for another cup of tea. What about you?'

Ten minutes later they nursed fresh mugs of tea, the dogs dozing beneath the table. The warmth of a soft body against her feet felt strangely comforting. Could she get a dog? Did Nikos have one in London?

She started to ask him, but he spoke first. 'What *is* wrong with Siena, MJ? How ill is she?'

Her heart lodged in her throat. If she told him, would he use that information to hurt Siena? Or their father, or her? He could circulate rumours, discrediting MJ's ability to lead the Mabel Group into the future. If clients and business partners thought her in danger of becoming seriously ill, opportunities could be lost. Big ones. Would he stoop to such tactics?

Her stomach gave a sickening lurch. If she told Niko, but Siena hadn't already confided in Christian, would Siena ever forgive her?

She recalled the expression in Siena's eyes when she'd had that dreadful fight with their father, and her heart plummeted. Siena could act tough and uncaring, but beneath the bluff she was sensitive and easily hurt. And she'd *always* preferred make-believe to reality. If she decided to bury her head in the sand now…

Acid burned her throat. If her sister continued to put off the tests she needed, she could lose a kidney. She could lose both kidneys. *She could die.*

'You don't want to tell me.' He stared at her, his eyes turning murky and his mouth hardening. 'You think I might use it against you and your family.'

'Would you?'

He opened his mouth, as if to utter an instant denial, but shut it again with a snap that had an ache stretching through her chest. He would—if it would give his family the upper hand over hers. The fact that the notion seemed to bring him little joy was no comfort at all.

'It's Siena's private information. It's for her to decide who should know. Not me.' Her heart pounded so hard it took a moment for her to push the words out. 'Would you…?'

'Would I…?'

'Would you give me Christian's mobile number?' Christian's volatile relationship with his father was well known. If he cared about Siena… well…surely that meant she could trust him to keep Siena's private information private? With Siena refusing to speak to her, she had left MJ little choice. 'I'd like to text him all he needs to know about Siena's condition—what he needs to know to keep her safe.'

He gave her the number without hesitation.

She composed a text to Christian—a long and comprehensive one—and sent it.

Please, God, let Siena forgive me.

She set down her phone. 'Thank you. No one else was prepared to part with his number.'

He nodded, then drummed his fingers against the table. 'What did Siena mean when she said that thing about your mother? About using her to make you feel better and less alone now that your mother's no longer here?'

MJ's stomach shrivelled to the size of a pea. Out in the garden they'd found an accord that had seemed auspicious, but that now felt like a lifetime ago. Suspicion and distrust once again reigned supreme. 'What did Christian mean when he said you were just like your father and grandfather?'

His lips pressed into a thin line.

He had no more intention of answering her question than she did his. 'Quid pro quo, Nikos,' she said softly.

Her words had his gaze spearing back. Slowly he nodded. 'I haven't shared the promised story about Christian yet.'

He hadn't.

'I don't know if it's a classic story, but have you finished your tea?'

'Yes.'

'Then follow me.'

He led her all the way to the upstairs attic. Although it was piled with boxes and discarded bits of furniture, it was still well kept and ordered. Sunlight filtered in from the rows of dormer windows that marched the length of the room, making the corners of the room appear shady rather than dark and sinister.

He led her across to the furthest corner and there, behind a couple of big wardrobes, she found a battered velvet sofa sitting on an old rug, and three mismatched occasional tables—one holding books, one displaying a collection of feathers and shells and the other one marked with coffee rings.

A large chest sat opposite the sofa beneath the window. Nikos nodded when she silently asked if she could look inside. It held a collection of boyhood treasures—a beaten up and evidently much-loved toy truck, a collection of bird eggs, comics, a football cap…

Her heart caught. *Siena's favourite scarf.*

Each item looked as if it'd been placed there in a certain order and with absolute precision, and she didn't have the heart to disturb a single thing. She lowered the lid and sat on it, and stared at Nikos, waiting.

He stared at the floor and she sensed he was miles away. She kept her hands folded in her lap and her mouth shut. She had no intention of rushing him, not when she could tell he was already half-regretting bringing her up here.

He gave a start and thumped down onto the sofa, waving a hand around the room. 'In the lead up to my parents' divorce, the family retreated here—away from the prying eyes of London.'

She nodded, understanding their need for privacy.

'During that time my parents…argued a great deal.'

He chose his words with care and she nodded again, reading the subtext. The Devon house had become a battlefield. 'I'm sorry.' She couldn't help it. Her heart ached for what Nikos and Christian must've suffered. She knew her father viewed them as mortal enemies, but she'd never been able to share his feelings…hadn't wanted to.

'It was especially hard on Christian. I was fourteen and understood what was going on. Christian was only ten, still a little boy. I was angry, hated what was happening to my family, but he…'

She rubbed a hand across her chest as pain flashed through his eyes. To witness the disintegration of his parents' marriage must have been so gut-wrenchingly distressing. Especially as a child.

'Christian was confused. Scared. Hurt.' He gestured around again. 'He created this little spot up here as a kind of haven. Surrounded himself with all of his favourite things and tried to forget what was happening downstairs.'

His favourite things? Siena's scarf now resided in the chest MJ sat upon. That had to be significant.

'It must've been the most awful time for you all. But Christian still managed to fashion this safe place for himself.' Good for him. If he'd been ten and Nikos fourteen… She worked it out. She and Siena would've been nine.

Was Christian now making a safe place for Siena somewhere? She crossed her fingers. 'This must've all been happening around the same time my mother died.'

His head came up. He stared at her with a strange expression in his eyes. 'Your mother died just before we came down here.'

'Worst year of my life,' she whispered. She thought of Siena and shivered. 'I had no idea you were going through an *annus horribilis* of your own.'

His gaze sharpened. With a smothered oath, he dropped his head to his hands, scrubbing his fingers back through his hair. Her heart thumped. She ached to go to him and put an arm around his shoulders. He looked so solitary and alone. But he wouldn't want her sympathy. He didn't want her friendship, and she couldn't force it on him, no matter how much she might want to.

Nikos bit back a curse. MJ didn't have a clue how her mother's death and his parents' divorce were related, did she? How the hell had her father managed to shield her sister and her from that knowledge? Even Christian knew part of it, if not the whole.

He pressed his fingers to his eyes. Not a lot of people had known about Graham's and Tori's affair. And nobody outside of their two families would know that, on the same day she'd had the car accident that had killed her, MJ's mother, Diana, had been driving to Graham's and Tori's rendezvous location to discover if what she'd been told that afternoon was true—whether her husband and Tori were having a torrid affair. It *had* all happened a long time ago. MJ had only been nine.

He lifted his head and forced in a breath. Over the years, in idle moments, he'd sometimes won-

dered how MJ had dealt with the knowledge, how
she'd coped with it. He'd wondered about how
much she must hate his parents—his mother for
the affair and his father for telling Diana about
it. That seemed almost laughable now. She hadn't
coped because she hadn't had a clue.

If he wanted to hurt her, he now had the perfect weapon.

An image of MJ with Rufus and Seth in the
garden rose through him. The determined chin
that hadn't quite hidden the tremble of her bottom
lip, the tears that had risen in her eyes when he'd
narrated the dogs' histories of abuse and neglect.

He didn't want to hurt her. *Damn it!* She wasn't
the hardened nemesis he'd created in his mind.
She wasn't the kind of woman who'd stop at nothing to contrive his downfall. MJ was savvy and
smart, but she was also kind and brave. And she
loved too many things. A corner of his heart trem-
bled for her. He had no intention of being the one
to reveal the ugly truth. It'd probably be best all
round if that particular truth remained buried.

'I'm sorry you had to go through all of that,
Nikos. I'm sorry it was so hard.'

'It wasn't your fault, MJ.' And for the first time
he felt the truth of that right down to his very
bones. She was no more to blame than he was.
He'd scoffed when she'd said she wanted to bring
the feud to an end…

But he wasn't an idiot. He knew his father, his

grandfather, her father—none of them would ever let it go. But the previous generations couldn't live forever. He couldn't imagine a time when the Constantinoses and Mabels would ever be friends, but he was starting to envisage a world where they weren't mortal enemies either.

'You've gone very quiet.'

He snapped out of his thoughts.

She glanced round again and smiled. 'Christian made a pleasant nest up here.'

He had. 'It was supposed to be his secret spot, but I found him up here one day.' When he'd been searching for a place where his parents' fighting wouldn't reach him. 'He'd found a clutch of baby starlings that had been blown from their nest. He'd been keeping them up here in a box with towels and a hot-water bottle, feeding them on condensed milk.' He bit back a sigh. 'They died of course. Damn near broke his heart.'

Her lips parted. 'What did you do?'

'We buried them, and the next day I searched high and low until I found a rabbit kitten. I gave it to him and told him how to look after it.'

'Did it survive?'

'It did, much to Mr Digby's disgust. He had no use for wild rabbits, but he built a hutch for it all the same once it grew too big for us to keep locked up in the attic.'

She laughed and it lightened something inside him. 'What a lovely big brother you were.'

They stared at each other for a long moment and he felt the same strange pull he always felt whenever he looked at her—as if something in him recognised something in her. Up here in the dim intimacy of the attic, the pull grew keener, stronger.

He stood and paced to the window. It'd meant drawing closer to her, but at least he'd been able to break eye contact. Down below Mrs Digby pegged laundry on the line. He drew the scent of vanilla deep into his lungs. 'This room served its purpose, but I doubt Christian ever comes up here any more.'

'Then you'd be wrong.'

He swung towards her.

She stood and lifted the lid of the chest, gesturing for him to look. 'See that blue and pink scarf there? That's Siena's favourite scarf. It's pure silk, hand-printed, and cost her an absolute packet. She treasures it. It's not the kind of thing she'd ever accidentally leave behind.'

His gaze drilled into hers. 'You think Christian took it?'

She rolled her eyes. 'No, Nikos, I don't think your brother is a thief.'

Of course she didn't. 'Sorry, I—'

'I suspect she gave it to him.'

'Why? It's not like he can wear it.'

'For an extremely clever man, you can be really dense sometimes.'

He wanted to take offence, but her smile removed any sting.

'It's obviously a love token. Haven't you ever done that?'

'No.' He frowned. 'Have you?'

'Of course I have.' She stared at the scarf. 'But not as an adult. I hardly think giving Bertie Stevens my princess ring and tiara set really counts. Though he did give me his red fire engine. With hoses that actually worked. So maybe it was true love after all.'

He snorted at her nonsense. A love token? Reaching into the trunk, he pulled out the scarf.

The air whistled between MJ's teeth. 'That's... it's an invasion of privacy.'

She could bet her life it was, but a Constantinos and Mabel sharing love tokens was an absolute disaster. He needed to nip this little romance—if that was what it was—in the bud ASAP. He held the scarf but made no move to unfold it. 'There's something wrapped in it.'

MJ pursed her lips and rolled her shoulders. 'Go on, then.' She nodded, gnawing on her bottom lip.

Very carefully, he unwrapped it. MJ said the scarf was precious to her sister. He didn't want Siena and Christian forming an attachment, but that didn't mean he wanted to treat MJ's sister's property with disrespect either.

MJ craned her neck. 'What is it?'

He held the photo frame towards her. A picture of Siena and Christian beamed from it, heads close together and arms around each other. She took it and ran a finger over Siena's face. 'She looks so happy.'

His throat tightened. So did Christian.

She nodded at the velvet ring box clenched in his hand. 'What do you have there?'

'This is the box that holds my maternal grandmother's engagement ring. I have a similar box with my paternal grandmother's engagement ring. They're family heirlooms. Meant for our future brides.'

'Engagement ring?' MJ took Siena's scarf from his unresisting fingers. 'Is the ring still inside?'

He didn't want to depress the little silver latch. He didn't want to know. He wished he'd left the scarf where it was. He wished they hadn't come here. Steeling himself, he opened it...and then held it towards her.

'Empty.' She tottered over to the sofa and sat. Lifting the scarf to her face, she inhaled, as if searching for a trace of her sister there. 'Well, that changes things.'

'How?' His voice sounded harsh and angry in the still air, but he couldn't temper it.

'Because they're obviously in love.'

He strode across to the sofa and sat too, choking back the torrent of savage words clamouring at the back of his throat. She didn't deserve his anger. 'This can't happen, MJ. A marriage between Christian and Siena would tear my family apart. I *won't* let that happen.'

'You're saying your father and grandfather would sooner cut Christian off—disown him—than accept a Mabel into the family?'

That was exactly what he was saying.

'But surely when they see how much Christian loves her…? And when they actually meet Siena…'

'You're deluding yourself if you think your father will be any different.'

'You're wrong. We can make them all see sense and—'

'Just because you want that to be true doesn't make it so!'

The force of his words echoed into every corner of the vast space, bouncing off every box and item of discarded furniture. Her head rocked back and the shock in her eyes had his hands clenching.

'This doesn't have to be a tragedy.' He did what he could to moderate his voice. 'We'll find them and talk sense into them. It's that simple.'

'Not a tragedy?' Her voice rose. 'You have to be joking, right? Our two families have Shakespeare written all over them.' She shot to her feet, hands clenched. 'I'm not going to let your father or grandfather—' she hesitated '—or my father destroy Siena *or* Christian.'

Damn, she was magnificent.

'If my father forces me to choose between him and Siena—' her throat bobbed '—I'll choose Siena, because she and Christian have done nothing wrong. Who will you choose, Nikos?'

A stone lodged in his chest and he couldn't speak.

Her eyes widened at whatever she saw reflected in his face and she took a step back.

He didn't want her looking at him with such appalled disillusion. He was a Constantinos! What did she expect? He forced himself to his feet. 'My father and grandfather have both suffered enough. I'll do all I can to protect them from further heartache. They have made many sacrifices for our family already. It's Christian's turn to make a sacrifice.'

'Do you not care about breaking their hearts?'

'Of course I care!' He slashed a hand through the air. 'But broken hearts mend.'

'Do they *really*?' That pointed chin hitched up, angled in challenge. 'Tell that to your grandfather and my great-aunt because I doubt they'd agree.'

Her words chilled him.

She sat again, folded the scarf, set the frame on top and plucked the ring box from his fingers.

'What are you doing?'

She snapped a photo of it all with her phone. 'I think we should let Siena and Christian know what we found, don't you? It's the decent thing to do.'

His stomach clenched even tighter, but he gave a curt nod. Hopefully the shock of it would pull Christian from his current romantic haze and make him realise the futility of continuing an engagement with Siena.

'Oh, and look.' Her phone buzzed and she turned it towards him. 'I have an incoming call from Freddy Smythe. This should be good.'

What the hell...?

She pressed her phone to her ear. 'Hello, Freddy.'

She listened to whatever he had to say and then her eyebrows rose. 'Hold on. I'm putting you on speaker phone.'

CHAPTER SIX

'REPEATING FOR THE benefit of your companion's ears,' Freddy said with an archness that set MJ's teeth on edge. Could he have made the word *companion* sound any more suggestive? 'I know where Christian and Siena are.'

She and Nikos shared a look as she set the phone on top of an abandoned chest of drawers. His distaste matched hers.

'Playing games again, Freddy?' Nikos folded his arms.

'Dastardly ones,' Freddy agreed with infuriating cheerfulness. 'And, just so we're clear, the information doesn't come free.'

'Of course it doesn't,' she drawled. What a piece of work he was. 'What's the asking price these days for selling out one's friends?'

If her dig perturbed him, he didn't let on. Nikos's scowl turned ferocious.

'My two cousins, Joey and Merrilee Withers, are currently between jobs. I want you to find placements for them somewhere in your oh-so-vast business empires.'

His request made her frown. Merri was a sweet girl, and MJ could find a place for her at Mabel's easily enough if she was serious, but...

Nikos raised an eyebrow. 'Why would you ask for something so selfless, Freddy?'

Exactly! How on earth could she and Nikos be so in tune in their reactions to Freddy and so at odds in relation to Christian and Siena?

'It's not selfless!' Freddy snorted. 'Let's just say it would suit my purposes to have my uncle feeling warmly towards me at the moment.'

Nikos raised an eyebrow and MJ nodded, pointing at herself and mouthing, "Merrilee."

'Very well,' Nikos said. 'Have Joey visit my office on Monday, and Merrilee visit MJ's.'

'Make it tomorrow and you have yourself a deal.'

MJ rolled her eyes. 'Fine, Freddy, it's a deal. Now tell us where Siena and Christian are.'

'Switzerland.'

Nikos pursed his lips. She stared at them. An indentation rested above the cupid's bow of his top lip. The bottom lip swelled fractionally fuller. Her mouth dried. Those lips looked firm and generous. They looked like the kind of lips that knew how to kiss a woman.

She wrenched her gaze away, her pulse echoing in her ears.

'They've gone to some medical clinic or health farm.'

Her head snapped up.

'What's the name of this facility?' Nikos demanded.

'Haven't a clue.'

Damn.

Nikos glared at the phone. 'You said you knew where they were.'

'I do! In as much as it's a medical centre in Switzerland.' He hesitated. 'Geneva, I believe. All it'll take is a bit of research on your part to track them down. You're now closer to finding them than you were before my call. So don't forget the deal!'

Nikos waved an impatient hand in the air. 'Yes, yes.'

'So what's the skinny? They both looked healthy enough to me. Is someone trying to dry out or—?'

'Goodbye, Freddy.' MJ ended the call.

Nikos paced to the window and back. 'The man is a worm.'

'He's worse than a worm. He's an amoeba on a worm.'

'Looks like we're going to Switzerland.'

'It does indeed.'

They drove back to London that afternoon and were booked on flights first thing the following morning. A medical facility… Had Siena gone to a clinic seeking treatment?

The knots that twisted MJ tight loosened a fraction. While Freddy obviously didn't know what was wrong with Siena, surely this must mean that Christian did? That he hadn't just deleted her text without reading it.

She crossed her fingers as she marched through London's Gatwick airport. If Siena and Christian were in love, then surely her sister had confided everything to him anyway? Wouldn't she do everything she could to ensure they had a rosy future full of promise ahead of them and not throw it all away in a blaze of glory?

She spotted Nikos across the concourse. Despite her best efforts, her pulse did a funny little dance. *Deep breaths*. It'd be foolish to trust him or expect too much from him.

While he might be a man who kept his word, she knew now what Christian had meant when he'd accused him of being just like his father and grandfather. Nikos gave too much credence to their families' feud, gave it too much power. The fact he had every intention of rupturing Christian's and Siena's relationship told her that.

How much influence did he have with his brother? Would his pressure and emotional blackmail succeed? Her heart quailed at the thought. If Siena loved Christian...

She set her jaw. She'd promised him the Ananke necklace. Nothing more. He sure as heck wasn't getting her co-operation in breaking up Siena and Christian, and he'd discover she could be a formidable opponent. She *would* bring all of her powers of persuasion to bear on their siblings. They *would* get her support. She wouldn't stand idly by and let anyone break Siena's heart.

'You're looking particularly martial today, MJ,' Nikos said when she reached his side.

If she hadn't already come to a standstill, she'd have tripped and stumbled at the expression in his eyes. They held real pleasure. Was that at seeing her? Her stomach turned to mush in the space of a heartbeat.

Oh, for heaven's sake. She swallowed and forced her lips into a semblance of a smile. 'Just eager to finally clap eyes on our pair of fugitives.'

'We're boarding at gate eighteen. I suggest we head straight on through and grab coffees on the other side.'

'Excellent plan. I—'

'Ms Mabel and Mr Constantinos?'

They both automatically turned and a camera flash immediately went off in their faces. The press. MJ bit back a rude word and smoothed out her features. Beside her Nikos did the same, but she sensed the tension coiling him up tight.

'Rumour has it the two of you have been spending a lot of time in each other's company recently. Would you like to comment?'

'No.' Nikos took her arm and started marching her towards the nearest check-in counter.

'Aw, have a heart. It's a slow news day and my editor is busting my—'

Nikos swung round. 'Mind your language around the lady!'

The reporter raised both hands in surrender and a shaft of mischief trickled through MJ. Mischief and something a little darker. She gently disengaged her arm from Nikos's grasp. 'Mr Constantinos and I are currently in secret negotiations.'

The reporter's eyes lit up at that juicy titbit. 'What kind of negotiations?'

'If we told you,' Nikos inserted smoothly, 'They wouldn't be secret any more, would they?'

He marched her through check-in with a speed that had her fighting back a laugh.

'Damn it, MJ! What the hell were you thinking?' he bit out when they were finally out of earshot. 'You made it sound like…'

She raised an eyebrow.

He raked a hand through his hair. 'My father is going to have a fit when he hears about this.'

Her grin widened. 'Mine too.'

His hand dropped back to his side. 'That's why you…?'

She nodded.

'You could've warned me,' he grumbled, following as she led the way to the business-class lounge.

'I could hardly warn you when I didn't know such an irresistible opportunity was going to present itself, could I? Besides, you've dealt with the press before. You're a man who can think on his feet. Don't worry, you looked as debonair and sophisticated as ever.'

His scowl deepened and she realised she'd pushed him a bit further than she'd meant to.

'I don't care how I looked,' he ground out. 'I care—'

'About your father,' she finished when he broke off. 'And your grandfather,' she added. 'And you don't want them catching wind of what we're up to. Or what Christian and Siena are up to.'

His silence spoke volumes.

She hauled in a breath, but he spoke before she could. 'You seem to think my wanting to spare them anxiety is a crime.'

'What I want to know is why they should be spared any worry whatsoever when it's they who continue to cling to this stupid feud. I'm starting to think the feud matters more to them than anything else—more than Christian and Siena's happiness, for example. Doesn't that seem wrong to you?'

She wanted to stir them all up—her father, his father and grandfather—and make them face the ugliness of being at daggers drawn, for bequeathing that *hatred* to their children.

'We're not going to agree on this, MJ, so just drop it.'

Something flashed in his eyes, something she

didn't understand. It sent unease spiralling through her. Was there something she didn't know?

Was his father in bad health? In which case she certainly understood his desire to shield the older man. She passed him her hand luggage. 'Find us somewhere comfortable to sit. I'll grab us coffees while you ring your father and make up some story about me simply trying to create mischief.'

MJ ticked off the last of the clinics that Siena's doctor had recommended she check out—ones the doctor thought might be of use to her sister. Her stomach clenched. Siena wasn't in any of them.

'What now?' Nikos asked.

'We head back to the hotel, I suppose.'

Neither of them spoke during the twenty-minute drive back to their hotel.

He followed her into her suite, his face a study in frustration. She fell onto the sofa, her shoulders slumping, and waved him to the bucket seat opposite.

Those dark eyes burned as they surveyed her. 'Don't give up, MJ. We'll find them yet. I made you a promise, didn't I?'

This was their second full day in Switzerland, tonight would be their third night but, despite their best efforts, they were no closer to finding Siena and Christian than when they'd started. What was more, none of Nikos's or her combined contacts in Switzerland had uncovered any news of note, and that in itself was astonishing.

Where on earth could Siena be?

Nikos had promised to help her find her sister, and he'd been trying. Hard. They both had. But it was becoming increasingly clear that their siblings didn't want to be found. And the trail was going cold.

She snatched up her phone when it rang, and then bit her lip as she read the caller ID. 'It's my father.'

Nikos immediately rose. 'I'll give you some privacy.'

'Nonsense,' she returned as crisply as she could, though her heart had started to hammer against her ribs. 'I don't expect this to take long, and we need to come up with a new plan.'

She lifted the phone to her ear. 'Hello, Father.'

'What are you up to?' The older man exploded.

'I'm fine, thank you,' she sing-songed. 'And you?'

She could practically hear his teeth grind together. 'Listen to me—'

'Have you made things right with Siena yet? I told you I wouldn't speak to you until you did. And I meant it.'

'Is it true you're with Nikos Constantinos?'

She let the silence stretch for a beat too long. She wanted her father anxious and uneasy. 'Have you spoken to Siena?' she repeated.

'Listen to me, MJ.' A new urgency entered his voice. 'There are things you don't know about the Constantinos family.'

'There are things you don't know about Siena,' she shot back. She knew which of those two issues he should be paying attention to.

'Do not trust Nikos Constantinos!'

She wasn't playing this game. She ended the call without uttering another word and sent all her calls to voicemail.

Nikos winced. There wasn't an ounce of triumph in his eyes. 'I'm sorry. That didn't sound as if it went well.'

'Drink?' She rose and lifted the brandy decanter, but he pointed to the mineral water instead. She poured two glasses, added ice and lime.

'He told you not to trust me, didn't he?'

'Of course he did. No doubt the same way your father told you not to trust me.'

She sipped her water. He did the same.

'He told me there are things I don't know,' she said.

His gaze immediately slid away and her heart thump-thumped.

'Right, so that's obviously true then, but...'

Nikos met her gaze again.

'I don't care. These hostilities—all of this bitterness—it has to stop.'

* * *

Nikos stared at MJ, at the resolution in those clear green eyes and the jut of her chin, and a burn started up at the centre of him.

She'd meant it when she'd said she wanted to bring an end to their families' hostilities, but her father was right. There were things she didn't know. Things that would hurt her.

Things that would make her as bitter as his father and hers.

Things that would make her as bitter as Nikos himself.

The thought of her disillusionment, of all of that warmth and light diminishing...

He paced across the room.

'Nikos?'

'This resolution of yours to fix things between our families.' He swung around. 'It could backfire, you know.' He pressed his lips together so hard they started to ache. 'Don't sacrifice yourself for it, because it won't be worth it.'

For the first time that day, she smiled. A real smile. One that slid in between his ribs and had him wishing for...

He didn't know! But he had to battle an entirely inappropriate and overwhelming tenderness—a sweetness and warmth that was as seductive as a blazing fire in the hearth on a cold, cold day. A warmth that wanted to possess him wholly and completely.

'Careful,' she teased, 'or you'll find yourself friends with me before you know it.'

He shook his head, unable to hide his smile. Despite his best intentions, it felt as if he and MJ were already friends. The woman could make him laugh when he least expected it. And the last four days had shown him that they were on the same page in so many ways. It was strange how so many of their values aligned. His lips twisted. Except the people who mattered. Such as their families.

A friendship might be forming, but the moment he separated Christian from her sister any amity between them would end. He'd seen enough evidence of her devotion to Siena to know that.

He braced himself against the weight that settled on his shoulders. It was an effort to fight the urge to close his eyes and sleep for a week.

'You know what, Nikos?'

He jerked his attention back.

'Freddy Smythe is a real weasel.'

'He is.' He moved back and planted himself in his seat. She was right. They needed to come up with a strategy to move forward. He needed to start thinking smart again, not mooning for impossible things.

'What was it you called him before—a toad?'

Her meaning sank in and he bit back something rude and succinct. 'You think he lied and sent us on a wild goose-chase?'

'Don't you?'

Damn the man. 'When I get my hands on him…'

'I think Siena and Christian put him up to it.'

He leaned forward. *'What?'*

'Think about it. The only part of Freddy's information that lent it any validity whatsoever was the mention of the medical clinic.'

'That and the fact he extorted something from us in return for the information.'

'But it wasn't something that would harm him personally if we were to renege.' She cocked her head to one side. 'I'll still trial Merri. I know why she was let go at her previous job and I don't like it. Her manager passed the buck and she took the blame.'

He stared at her. 'Are you a one-man crusader?'

'Woman,' she corrected.

'I suppose you want me to give Joey the promised trial too?' He scowled. 'What do you know of him?'

'He's young…been partying too hard and giving his father headaches. I suspect he just needs a bit of direction.' She suddenly grinned. 'If he doesn't pull up his socks, you could always have him cool his heels at your Reykjavík hotel.'

That made him laugh. 'Okay, fine, I'll trial him, but I'm making no promises beyond that.'

Her grin was the only thanks he needed.

She sobered again. 'Back to my original point,

though. Siena had to have told Freddy what to say to throw us off the scent.'

She was right.

'There is one silver lining in all of this.'

'I can't see it myself, MJ. You might need to help me out.'

'Freddy might be a toad, but at least he didn't betray them. I hate to think of either Siena or Christian's friends selling them out.' When he didn't say anything, she frowned. 'Don't you?'

This woman was going to be the death of him. He rubbed a hand over his face. 'Were you born an optimist?'

Something sad floated through her eyes before it was blinked away, replaced instead with her natural smile. 'I think being aware of the things in your life you should be grateful for is more conducive to happiness than brooding about everything that's wrong.'

Like the feud?

Still, he had to admit she had a point. 'Are there any other silver linings to this situation you'd like to share?'

Her eyes filled with mischief. 'Getting to know you has been mostly fun. And definitely interesting. I always knew I'd like you.'

He wanted to laugh the words off, deflect them, but beneath her teasing he sensed she was deadly serious and it knocked the breath clean from his body. Something fierce, hot and sweet pooled in the space left behind, and he didn't know what to do with it. 'Marjorie...' He halted, not sure what to say.

'Ooh, Nikos Constantinos at a loss for words?' Her lips kinked upwards and those mossy-green eyes sparkled almost emerald. 'I bet that doesn't happen very often.'

It took a super-human effort to fight an answering smile.

She sobered. Shadows replaced the sparkles. 'So, in your world view, not only can't Siena and Christian become romantically involved but we can't be friends either?'

He rubbed that hand over his face again, wishing he'd chosen a brandy instead of mineral water. 'I thought you had enough friends already.'

'Oh, Nikos.' She stared at him with the kind of pity one normally reserved for stray dogs and crying babies. 'One can never have too many friends.'

She leapt up and strode around the room. He followed her movements, finding them oddly and soothingly hypnotic. Some critical inner voice told him she didn't move with any more grace than other women he knew, that her figure wasn't finer or her hair shinier, but the sight of her held him spellbound. And the longer he watched, the greater was the hunger that started gnawing at the centre of him.

He and MJ friends?

It shocked him how much the idea appealed. Maybe once the Ananke necklace was where it belonged—in the Constantinos family vault—he and MJ could become friends. Maybe between them they could start to heal the breach that two generations of hate and hostility, betrayal and bitterness, had created.

'There's another silver lining, of course.' MJ spoke quietly, but when she spun back to face him her eyes had grown serious and full of intent. 'Freddy's mention of the medical clinic, even though he used it as a blind, has to mean Christian knows about Siena's medical condition. Either Siena has confided in him, or he read my text.'

What the hell was wrong with Siena? And was MJ unwell too?

He scanned her for signs of illness and fatigue. Admittedly, she looked a little tired, but her colour had improved over the last couple of days. And her energy levels hadn't flagged until this afternoon when she'd realised they'd been duped. His had too, though.

His hands clenched and unclenched. He'd not seen her touch so much as a single drop of alcohol. Although she'd said she loved bacon and eggs, toast and pastries, she'd not eaten anything like that since leaving Devon. She mostly ate vegetables, salads and a little lean meat. She drank tea relatively freely but limited herself to one cup of coffee a day. For the rest of it she drank water—still and sparkling.

Things inside him pulled tight.

'Nikos?'

He blinked.

'Wouldn't you agree?'

'About what?'

She rolled her eyes, as if realising she'd been talking to thin air. 'If Christian knows about Siena's condition, he'll do everything he can to take care of her?'

'Not a doubt in my mind,' he said immediately, because she needed the reassurance.

He flashed back to the empty ring box. If Christian loved Siena, he'd move heaven and earth to make sure she had everything she needed.

Pressing fingers to his eyes, he counted to three before dragging them away and meeting MJ's gaze. 'What's wrong with Siena, MJ? How serious is it?'

She stared back with bruised eyes. Striding across, he closed his fingers about her shoulders, careful to keep his touch gentle. 'You have my word I will never use this information to hurt you and your family, but you're identical twins— identical DNA. Are you ill too?'

Should he be seeking medical attention for her? Was she risking her health not only to find her sister but to bring their families' feud to an end?

The feud wasn't worth that kind of sacrifice.

She chewed her bottom lip. 'Perhaps we should sit.'

How bad was this?

He led her to the sofa but, rather than returning to his original seat, he eased down beside her. He might be crowding her—the sofa was only small—but he refused to relinquish his hold on her hand.

'First of all...' She dragged in a breath and sent him the smallest of smiles that would've felled any remaining barriers he'd still had in place. 'Identical twins' DNA is identical at the moment of conception—same egg, same sperm—but, the moment the fertilised egg divides, slight changes in each twin's environment means our DNA is no longer identical. Similar, yes, but not identical.'

He mulled that over and nodded. 'Okay.'

'Both Siena and I have polycystic kidney disease. It's a hereditary condition and we have the recessive type, which is less common.' One slim shoulder lifted. 'The severity of the disease varies from person to person. It's possible I could go through my whole life without it ever causing me a problem.'

He caught a slight stress on 'my' and 'me'. 'What happens when it doesn't remain dormant?' Was that even the right word?

'Worst-case scenario is kidney failure.'

Hell! That meant...

She winced and with a start he realised how tightly he gripped her hand. He immediately loosened his hold and worked hard to keep his voice gentle. 'Are Siena's kidneys failing?'

'I don't know. Her last round of test results threw up some early indications that all might not be well—higher than normal blood pressure, traces of blood in her urine.'

'She's aware of this?'

She swallowed and nodded. Tears welled in her eyes.

He wrapped an arm around her shoulders and pulled her against his chest. How could Siena be so thoughtless? She had to know how much her twin would worry. 'We'll find her, MJ. I promise.'

He could see now why she'd been prepared to trade the Ananke necklace for his assistance. Besides her sister's health, its importance faded into insignificance.

She softened against him and her perfume rose up all around him in a sweet cloud that had his every sense sharpening—making him minutely conscious of the warm weight of her against his chest, the softness of her hair against his cheek and the strange sense of *déjà vu* that settled over him. As if she'd been in his arms exactly like this, and nothing had ever felt quite so right.

He swallowed and made his voice as matter-of-fact as he could. 'If Christian is aware of Siena's health issues, he will look after her.'

With a sigh, she lifted her head, and he immediately missed the weight and warmth of her. 'Except we're not a hundred per cent sure he does know. And you think him gullible and easily manipulated by a woman he considers himself in love with.'

It was true. 'While you're worried the news of her latest test results has sent Siena into a spin and made her reckless.'

She hadn't said as much, but he realised that was what she'd feared from the very first. His heart burned—for Siena and Christian, but mostly for MJ.

'There's something I haven't told you,' she whispered.

He brushed her hair from her face and let his hand linger against her cheek a moment longer than he should've. 'What's that?'

Had he imagined that she'd arched into his touch?

'I think Siena deliberately picked that fight with my father. They're opposites—he's practical, she's artistic; he's focused, she's dreamy; he's hard-headed, she's soft-hearted. You get the picture. They love each other but struggle to understand one another.'

While MJ understood them both. And was devoted to them both.

'I think she deliberately enraged him as much

as she could, and then I think she picked a fight with me.'

Frown lines marked her brow and he wanted to smooth them out. MJ was the kind of woman who deserved sunshine, sweet pastries and smiles, not this gut-wrenching worry and heartache.

'She knew I'd try to play peace maker, and I think she made a deliberate decision to act as offended and outraged as possible by it.'

It was his turn to frown. 'Why would she do that?'

'To alienate us both.'

He still didn't understand. A single tear spilled onto her cheek and a groan rose through him. 'MJ, please don't cry.' He wasn't sure he could bear it.

She forced her lips into the semblance of a smile. It didn't help. Had he ever seen a sadder smile?

'My father is a match. His kidney was always going to whichever one of us needed it first. Of course, he's only allowed to give one, so…'

When her meaning hit him, his heart stopped. 'You think she's run away so…?'

'She always credits me with saving her life against the dog that day. I think this is her returning the favour.'

Siena had run away so that she wouldn't take the kidney MJ might one day need. While MJ…

Nikos saw in that moment the sisters' devotion for each other.

She pulled in a ragged breath. 'I bet she hasn't told Christian that.'

Resolve crystallised inside him. 'Marjorie, I promise you we'll find them.' He'd move heaven and earth to make that happen.

Her breath hitched as if she'd read that thought in his face. And then he realised he'd been cradling her face and tracing her bottom lip with his thumb, his body unconsciously betraying his desire for her.

He should move away, apologise.

Reaching up, she pressed her hand to his cheek. 'Dear Nikos,' she whispered, a matching desire flaring in her eyes. No fear accompanied that desire, even though he was a Constantinos and the last man she should ever trust. Instead, awe, wonder and a building excitement turned her eyes a brighter shade of green. He found himself drowning in them and never wanting to surface. 'Such a noble face,' she murmured.

He knew what she was really telling him was that she thought *him* noble. In that moment he was helpless to stop his mouth from descending to hers. Their lips instantly shaped themselves to the other's in a fit so perfect it sent sensation roaring through every nerve ending.

Dear God.

Her mouth opened and so did his. It felt as if he

stood on the edge of a cliff about to take flight. He was glorying in the freedom of it, the sense that anything was suddenly possible, when a shrill ringing tore through the moment and had them jumping apart.

Dazed eyes met dazed eyes. Mere seconds had passed but everything had changed.

With a muttered oath, he grabbed his phone and glanced at the caller ID. Blowing out a breath and grimacing, he brought it to his ear. 'Grand-father.'

CHAPTER SEVEN

NIKOS SWUNG AWAY to take his phone call and MJ did what she could to get her breathing back under control. She didn't have a hope in Hades of tempering the wild race of her pulse, though. That kiss had been…

She marched over to the bar fridge and poured herself another mineral water, more aware than ever of the bedroom behind the nearby closed door.

The moment had been so brief, it barely qualified as a kiss, and yet its impact reverberated through her like an earthquake, shifting the ground beneath her feet.

She turned to find Nikos surveying her. His gaze immediately slid away. She knew that barely nothing kiss continued to reverberate through him too. He'd been just as dazed as she when they'd broken apart.

She gulped her mineral water but it did nothing to cool the fevered, half-formed hopes that whipped through her like wisps of cloud scudding before a spirited breeze. In ordinary circumstances, if she'd ever experienced something like that she'd be breathless with excitement, anticipation…hope.

But circumstances were far from ordinary.

And she'd never imagined sharing a moment like *that* with Nikos Constantinos. She'd be a fool to let it happen again.

Oh, she liked him well enough, and to a certain extent she trusted him. For years now she'd surreptitiously watched him whenever she'd found herself in the same room, read whatever the newspapers printed about him, undeniably fascinated with the man. But she'd always put it down to the bad blood between their two families and her fantasies of finding a way to heal the breach.

Had she been lying to herself all these years? Had her fascination been due to something more primal? Had it been due to an attraction she hadn't wanted to acknowledge?

She strode to the window and stared out at the street below—part of Geneva's old town, its cobblestones and quaint old-world shop fronts looking like something out of a fairy tale. She pressed her glass to her cheek.

She and Nikos had so much in common. They shared the same work ethic, took the same joy in their careers and found the same sense of satisfaction in it. He wasn't a playboy and she wasn't a party girl. Neither one of them was a player. And they were both devoted to their families.

On paper, they were perfect for each other.

If not for the feud.

If not for him buying into the feud, she told herself with blunt ruthlessness. She'd be an idiot to hide from that fact. If Nikos refused to tolerate a union between their siblings, he sure as hell wouldn't allow himself to fall for her.

That was the thing to remember.

And, even if the world turned upside down and he had a road-to-Damascus moment and wanted to embark on a romance with her, what if things didn't work out? What if it went bad? That would only cement the poor relations between their families, not heal them. And she wasn't risking more bad blood between the Mabels and Constantinoses.

'MJ?'

She turned, heat flaring in her cheeks when she realised it wasn't the first time he'd called her name. *Focus.*

He hesitated. 'About that kiss.'

The expression in his eyes almost broke her heart. She could challenge him, force him to acknowledge the attraction between them, but what good would it do?

She made herself smile. 'It barely deserves the title of a kiss. If we'd blinked we'd have missed it, it was so brief.'

He stared. 'So…you're okay with it?'

She frowned. Did *he* want to talk about it? 'Are you? Okay, I mean?'

'Of course.'

That was a no, then. He was just being polite.

'Emotions have been running high, Nikos. It's no excuse, but…'

His shoulders unhitched a fraction. 'I guess it's natural to search for a release valve when things get tense.' He grimaced. 'But that's not the ideal way to…'

'Heavens, no.' At least they agreed on that.

'I'm sorry, MJ. I—'

'Do you remember stumbling across me in the gardens at the Wallaces' golden anniversary party?' It had been noisy and crowded inside and she'd sneaked away to sit by the fountain. 'I was sixteen, so I guess you'd have been twenty-one.'

He hesitated, though whether it was because she'd thrown him with the change of topic, or because he had no idea what she was talking about, she couldn't tell.

'I knew who you were, of course, but it was the first time we'd ever come face to face.' She dragged in a breath but couldn't find a smile. 'I introduced myself to you and held out my hand, but you refused to shake it. Instead you turned on your heel and went back to the party without saying a word.' She rubbed a hand across her chest. 'You've no idea how much that hurt my feelings.' She'd gone home and cried. That was when the feud between their families had finally felt personal.

'I didn't mean to hurt your feelings, MJ.'

She glanced up. So, he did remember.

'Put yourself in my shoes. I was twenty-one and you were sixteen—' his lips twisted '—and looking an absolute picture.'

Had he thought her pretty?

'Besides the fact that our fathers were sworn enemies, no twenty-one-year-old should be found in what could be construed as a compromising situation with a teenage girl. If your father had seen...'

He broke off with a shake of his head.

She blinked. She hadn't thought about it in those terms. She'd just thought he'd hated her so much he'd refused to engage with her on any level.

'I'm sorry I hurt you. If I could go back to that day, I'd shake your hand and tell you it was nice to meet you and then leave. I'm sorry I didn't do that.'

Suddenly she could smile without any effort at all. 'See, that's an apology I'm happy to accept. But, as for the kiss that was barely a kiss, none is necessary.' She nodded at the phone in his hand. She didn't want to talk about the kiss any more. 'That was your grandfather?'

'I've been ordered to report for duty. He wants a face-to-face meeting.' His lips briefly twisted, but he schooled them almost immediately, as if he hadn't meant to betray his impatience.

'A face-to-face meeting?' On his private Greek island? Aunt Joan had been scathing about her former swain's romantic retreat, his dramatic exile from the real world. While he might have shunned society, he'd continued to be the puppet master controlling the strings of the Leto Group, nursing his sense of injury like some tragic Greek hero of old.

The very thought of him made MJ lose all patience. Another thought struck her. 'Christian and Siena aren't there, are they?' Was it possible they'd found an unlikely ally in Vasillios Constantinos? Now, that would be an interesting twist to the tale.

He shook his head. 'But—quote—' he made air quotes '—he has information.'

'Then why didn't he just give it to you over the phone?'

He remained silent and, while not a single muscle moved in his face, a shadow passed behind the dark brown of his eyes.

Slowly she nodded. 'He wants to impart to you, face-to-face, the importance of ensuring this thing between Siena and Christian doesn't develop into anything permanent.'

'Family is everything to my grandfather.'

'Not everything,' she returned. 'His love for his family isn't greater than nursing his sense of injury and resentment towards my family.'

'Which only makes him want to protect his family all the more. They're intertwined, MJ, and nothing anyone says will have him seeing that differently.'

'And so...what? You must be a slave to it as well?' She slashed a hand through the air. 'The man is as stubborn and wrong-headed as my great-aunt was.'

Nikos blinked and straightened. Behind the darkness of his eyes, she sensed his mind racing. 'Would you like to accompany me?'

She had no hope of hiding the way her eyes started from their sockets, but she immediately nodded in case he should change his mind and take the offer back. 'Yes please.'

One broad shoulder lifted. 'It was part of the deal we made—that I wouldn't ditch you somewhere or give you the slip.'

He was trying to justify the invitation, and she could see that was the line he meant to give to his grandfather, but what was his real reason?

And would she be able to discover it before they reached the island?

'You did,' she agreed. 'It would be contravening our agreement if you were to travel to your grandfather's without me.'

'And I've no intention of giving you the smallest loophole for not handing over the Ananke necklace at the end of all this.'

A stone lodged in her chest. Did he really care so much about the necklace? 'So, what's the plan?'

His eyes narrowed. 'What do you mean, *what's*

the plan? I love my grandfather. I've no intention of betraying or manipulating him.'

But he had an agenda. She sensed that much.

'Nikos?' She started to lift her eyes to meet his gaze, but her attention snagged on his lips. Everything inside her pulled tight. How she ached to…

The white line of his mouth pulled her up short. A pulse in his throat pounded and his eyes had gone too dark. She jerked herself back. What had they been talking about? *Oh, that's right.* 'I merely referred to our travel plans.'

'Oh.'

His gaze dropped briefly to her lips, heat gathered beneath her breast bone and she swore perspiration gathered between her breasts.

'We'll leave for Athens in the morning and I'll charter a yacht to the island.

She gave a nod because she wasn't sure she could speak.

'Have you sailed before?'

She took a gulp of lukewarm mineral water. It did nothing to dampen the heat rising through her. 'I sailed once, a long time ago, on Lake Windermere.'

'The island is only three hours from the mainland. I've made the trip on my own more times than I can count, so you won't be called on to crew. I was just curious. Can you swim?'

'Like a fish.' If she fell overboard, he wouldn't need to dive in to save her.

He rolled his shoulders. 'Did you want to go out for dinner tonight?'

He wasn't asking her on a date. They were simply stuck in the same city together, and he was being polite. 'I'm a little tired after all of our traipsing around. I was planning on ordering room service and getting an early night.'

For a moment she thought he might argue, but then he nodded. 'That's probably wise.'

All the fine hairs on her arms stood to attention at the way the words left his lips. Lips that looked as if they yearned to…

'I mean, it'll be a big day tomorrow, and we'll want to be fully rested. Plus, there's some work I need to get done.'

She didn't say a single word when he turned on his heel and left. She wanted nothing more than to fall face first on her bed and groan into the eiderdown. Instead she forced herself to fetch her phone. 'I need you to arrange for a courier to deliver a package to Athens airport,' she said to her PA. 'You'll find it in the safe.' She gave a description of the parcel. 'I'm afraid I need it first thing in the morning.'

Once she'd ended the call, she opened the door to her bedroom, fell face-down on her bed and groaned.

MJ didn't sleep well that night. Nikos didn't look any better rested the following morning either, which didn't help. She'd not been able to stop her mind from drifting to all the things they could've been doing instead—things that would have been far more fun. At least then she'd have felt she'd earned her sleepless night.

But they were foolish things, the things she and Nikos could've been doing, she told herself for the millionth time. They couldn't lead to anything permanent. And, with the best will in the world, those sorts of foolish things could lead to hurt feelings.

She'd vowed to her Aunt Joan and herself to do everything in her power to heal the rift between their two families. She couldn't do anything now that might jeopardise that. It'd be selfish and self-defeating. Besides, if Siena did truly love Christian, then MJ would do everything in her power to smooth the way for her sister, not make matters worse.

'I thought you said you were on a leave of absence,' Nikos said when she collected her parcel from the airport the next morning.

'I am.'

A smile touched his lips. 'And you call me a workaholic.'

'You are.'

'Pot.' He pointed to her and then himself. 'Kettle.'

She laughed. She couldn't help it. There was a subtle change in Nikos today. His step was lighter and his eyes brighter—and she couldn't prevent it from infecting her.

From the airport, they headed straight to the marina. He turned his phone towards her and pointed to a storm front showing on the screen. 'There's a storm forecast for this evening.'

She wrinkled her nose. 'I'm definitely a fair-weather sailor. I don't want to be tossed around like a cork on big seas in gale-force winds.'

'We'll be at my grandfather's island enjoying a cool drink by the time this hits.' Keen eyes raked her face. 'But I'll check with more experienced heads before we leave, just to make sure.'

'I'd appreciate that.'

Fifteen minutes later, he returned from the marina's main office. 'Common wisdom claims the storm will miss us completely.'

'I like the sound of that.'

'We might get a shower later this evening, but that's probably the worst of it.'

'Excellent.' She gestured to their yacht. 'What do you want me to do?'

He helped her on board and then pointed to a seat. 'What you can do, MJ, is take the weight off and enjoy the ride.'

She realised then the reason for his good mood—Nikos loved to sail. And, as she watched him navigate the boat out of the harbour, she discovered that she loved to watch him sail.

He looked at home on board this small yacht.

At one with the elements. Who would have guessed that beneath those immaculate business suits beat the heart of a man at home on the sea?

A brisk breeze filled their sails and they clipped along at a playfully brisk pace. She lifted her face to the sun and closed her eyes, enjoying the sound of splashing water, the cry of a sea bird and the scent of salt that seasoned the air.

'What do you think?' Nikos asked, turning from the wheel to smile down at her.

'It's glorious! It feels like...'

'Freedom.'

She nodded. 'I need to take up sailing.'

He grinned up at the sky. She stared at the strong, tanned column of his throat and a deep ache burrowed into her chest. He glanced back at her and very slowly he sobered, his eyes darkening. She didn't want the moment to end...

Don't be foolish.

She dragged her gaze away. Swallowed. 'Shouldn't you be keeping your eyes on the road?'

He didn't speak for a long moment, but she didn't dare glance at him again. 'There are drinks and a packed lunch down below if you want anything,' he finally said.

She nodded, but didn't speak, trying to find her earlier sense of serenity.

'Can I ask you something, MJ?'

She glanced up and gave a cautious nod.

'Why would Siena get sick now? You said there

are slight differences in your DNA, that environmental factors play a role.'

She fought a frown. Why did he want to know?

'For example, is being out here in the elements, or taking an unexpected dip in a cold sea or air travel likely to cause you any issues?'

Her heart turned over in her chest. She'd known he was a good man from the years she'd spent observing him, but those words confirmed it. He wanted to keep her safe, to prevent her from falling ill.

Nikos could feel the ticking of his heart as he waited for MJ to answer. If she caught a cold or chill would it set off her illness? What about stress? Or a shock—such as a bump on the head or unexpectedly falling off a yacht into the sea?

'When we were babies, Siena got a UTI that went undiagnosed and developed into a kidney infection. That's how we were initially diagnosed as having polycystic kidney disease in the first place. She suffered damage to her kidneys then.'

Damage MJ hadn't suffered.

'Our parents were always ridiculously vigilant after that, never letting the slightest high temperature go un-investigated.'

He didn't blame them. He couldn't imagine what it would be like to have something like that hanging over one's children's heads.

'We've had six-monthly check-ups ever since.

My doctor assures me that I could go to annual checks, but the six-monthly ones give my father some peace. And it seems such a small thing to do.'

She might be leading her father a merry dance now, but he could see she'd spare him any unnecessary anxiety about her health that she could.

His hands tightened on the wheel. How the hell could Siena frighten her family like this? He recalled what MJ had said to him yesterday about Siena not wanting to take their father's kidney in case MJ should ever need it. He rubbed a hand across his chest. What would he do in Siena's place?

She reached across and briefly clasped his arm. It was all he could do not to lift it to his lips. 'Stop looking so serious. Polycystic kidney disease can't be cured, but it can be treated.'

A kidney transplant was pretty extreme treatment!

'And, like I said, it might never become an issue for me.'

Having something like this affecting her had probably given her a very different view of mortality—about what was worth clinging to and what was worth letting go.

Such as the feud.

And maybe she was right. For so long, he'd had such a rigid view of the antagonism that existed between their families. There were reasons—

strong reasons—for bitterness on both sides. But, between them, could he and MJ begin to heal that breach and prevent it from impacting future generations?

If he had the Ananke necklace, it might be possible for him to reconcile his grandfather...

His fingers tightened on the wheel. If Christian truly loved Siena, *truly* loved her, nothing Nikos did or said would convince him to give her up. It would cause a rupture in their family unless Nikos found a way to reconcile his father and grandfather to the match.

But he needed to find his brother first before he raised any of that with the older generations. Christian and Siena could just be enjoying a harmless fling, a bit of fun that would eventually burn itself out. His lips thinned. Or it could just be Siena doing her best to estrange her father.

'And you don't know exactly how ill Siena is? Or if her kidneys are failing?'

A shadow passed over MJ's face and he wished he hadn't asked. She'd already told him she didn't know. 'All I can tell you is that the poor test results are an indication that something *might* be wrong, not that something *is* definitely wrong. She'll need further tests to know for sure. If something is wrong, though, she needs to start treatment ASAP.'

'Instead she's tripping the light fantastic with

my brother and giving you and your father heart attacks.'

'My father doesn't know about Siena's recent test results.'

Hadn't MJ told him?

'And if they were living the high life we'd have found them by now. No, they've gone to ground. Siena can do a brilliant job of ignoring reality. I have visions of them living in some wonderfully rustic farmhouse in Tuscany or the south of France, far from everyone and everything. I just hope their phones aren't lying at the bottom of a lake or well, or smashed into a thousand pieces. My worst nightmare is Siena collapsing and Christian not having a clue why.'

Things inside Nikos clenched tight. He knew Christian had said he'd never forgive him if he hired a PI, but...

'Quid pro quo?' MJ asked, before he could develop that line of thought further.

He glanced across. For someone who'd hardly ever been on a yacht, she looked remarkably at home.

And she'd felt utterly at home in his arms.

He did what he could to squash that unwelcome thought. He needed to cut all memory of their kiss from his mind. Which was easier said than done. That brief kiss had rocked the foundations of his world.

Which was exactly why he had to block it from his mind now.

'You want to ask me something?' *Please God, don't let it be about the kiss.*

'What's the real reason you invited me along to visit your grandfather? And does he know I'm accompanying you?

Ah. 'I haven't told him you're coming,' he said carefully. 'But he has a lot of...friends.'

He watched her mull that over. 'So someone from the marina has probably already reported in to him.'

Probably.

'That answers my second question, but what about the first?'

When he didn't answer immediately, she turned to stare out at the water. Evidently, if he didn't want to answer, she wasn't going to press him.

'Besides the fact that I enjoy your company?'

She swung back, eyes wide.

'And God help me...' his lips twisted '...but I do.'

She didn't laugh at him. Her eyes became warm and somehow gentle. 'And that's a bad thing? Because I'm a Mabel?'

He shrugged. 'That's how I once thought, but it's not how I feel now.'

A man could fall into those eyes.

He wrenched his gaze away. 'Obviously, I now realise you're not some scarlet woman out to destroy me, my family or my family's empire.' It seemed ludicrous to think he'd ever suspected such a thing.

She rubbed her hands together and sent him a teasing smile. 'Ooh, we're making progress.'

'I'd fallen into the habit of taking as gospel all that my father and grandfather had to say on the matter.' He scraped a hand across his jaw. 'They've fallen into the habit of believing the worst of your family and expecting the worst—and constantly bracing themselves against attack.'

But the Mabels hadn't made any such attack, and he could see now that they had no such intention. The death of MJ's mother had made them lose their appetite for such hostilities. And MJ didn't have revenge on her mind.

She wanted to mitigate and conciliate.

Because she doesn't know the truth.

A band squeezed his chest, making it hard to get air into his lungs. It was a truth better buried for everyone's sakes.

Better for whom?

He clenched his jaw. It wasn't his truth to tell.

'You're hoping that, in meeting me, your grandfather will get a different perspective on the situation?'

Her words came slowly, haltingly, and all he could do was shrug. 'I don't know if that's even possible.'

'You know what?' One corner of her generous

mouth lifted. 'That sounds like a challenge I'm definitely up for.' With a smile, she rose. 'Would you like a drink?'

She headed below deck to get drinks. 'Hey, it's really cute down here!'

But when she started up the ladder again, she halted, her smile freezing on her face. She said an unladylike word that had him swinging round, and he nearly swore himself. He caught himself in time. He didn't want to alarm her. The sky in the east had darkened to every shade of charcoal, black and dark green on the colour chart, and on cue a wind whipped up into his face. If he'd been on his own he'd have tried to outrun it, but a glance at MJ and the way she gnawed on her bottom lip put paid to that idea.

'I love disaster movies.' She handed him a bottle of water, her voice wobbling the tiniest bit. 'But at moments like these I wish I hadn't watched quite so many of them.'

That made him laugh. 'We're not going to run into disaster, MJ, I promise.' He took a swig of water before screwing the lid back on. 'As you're still finding your sea legs, we'll sit this one out. I don't want to give you a nasty bout of seasickness.'

'For which I'm grateful, but...' She glanced at the clouds that were rapidly advancing. 'How does one *sit it out* on the open sea?'

He handed her back the bottle of water and

reached beneath the seats for life jackets. He carefully placed one over her head and did up the ties. 'This is a precautionary measure only.' He pulled the other over his own head.

'Precautionary, huh?'

He curved his hands round her shoulders and squeezed lightly. 'Don't look so nervous. We're going to be fine. The weather was supposed to be coming from the south, not the east, so it's caught me on the hop.' He should have been paying more attention. 'See that island over there? We're going to anchor in its leeward side, which will protect us from the wind and let us ride out the storm in relative comfort.'

She followed the line of his finger. 'Can that little pile of rocks actually be called an island?'

He lifted his eyes heavenward. 'First a kiss isn't a kiss because it's too brief. And then an island isn't an island because from this distance it looks too small.'

Damn, he shouldn't have mentioned the kiss, but the consternation in MJ's eyes disappeared as her gaze lowered to his lips. Without thinking, he bent his head and captured her mouth in another blistering kiss.

Her mouth opened under his, not in surprise but in hunger. She tasted of honey and heat and felt like silk and springtime. Her fingers dug into his forearms and he nearly lost his mind then and there.

'Any dispute that was a real kiss?' he rasped out when he finally lifted his head, his breath sawing in and out of his lungs.

She touched her fingers to her lips, her eyes huge. 'None whatsoever.'

'So when I say that's an island…' The finger he pointed towards the island was far from steady.

'Then we'll agree it's an island.' Then she laughed, and he wanted to hear that sound again and again. 'What can I do to help?'

'I'll be quicker on my own but, if you want something to do, I can find a job for you.'

She glanced at the advancing storm front. 'Sometimes the wisest and most strategic move is to get out of the way and let the experts get on with it.'

Her words shouldn't have surprised him. He already knew she wasn't one of those people who needed to constantly prove themselves. And, although he knew she'd much rather keep busy, she refused to allow her fear to override her common sense.

'I'm guessing the best place to stay out of the way is…?' She pointed below deck and he nodded. 'And you'll shout if you need any help?'

'I promise. But, MJ, in half an hour we're going to be at anchor with the kettle on.'

Without another word she disappeared below deck and Nikos set sail for the little island, the wind whipping them along at a great rate of knots.

He made minor adjustments here and there, trying to choose the easiest, least bumpy route, but the entire time that kiss burned in his mind.

Why the hell had he kissed her?

He shouldn't have kissed her. It'd been a stupid thing to do.

And yet he couldn't find it in himself to regret it, not in the slightest. That kiss hadn't felt stupid. It had felt like a promise.

CHAPTER EIGHT

TRUE TO HIS WORD, within half an hour Nikos steered them into a sheltered cove and the noise of the wind and the bumpy seas gave way to a strange silence and odd calm.

MJ peered out of a porthole and huffed out a laugh, but whether in genuine amusement or despair she didn't know. It was just that the outside conditions perfectly mirrored her emotional state—tempestuous and wild, but momentarily encased in a pocket of calm.

Nikos had kissed her. *Again*. And she'd barely been able to think straight since. Maybe that had been the point. Maybe it'd been a deliberate strategy to stop her from worrying about the storm outside by creating an even greater storm inside her.

Her solitary half-hour had given her a chance to lecture herself. Remind herself how foolhardy it would be for Nikos and her to act on the attraction flaring between them. Neither of them entered into sexual relationships lightly. If they threw caution to the wind and acted on impulse, feelings would become engaged.

And there was no room for her in Nikos's world. His loyalty to his family would always prevent it. Feelings *would* get hurt.

She gnawed on her bottom lip. Yet she sensed he'd started to consider the possibility of a ceasefire between their two families. For his own sake, or for Christian's?

Siena and Christian...

She pondered again Freddy's mention of the medical clinic. Maybe her sister wasn't being as reckless as she feared. Maybe Siena was seeking the treatment she needed.

If a truce could be brokered between the families—for Siena's and Christian's sakes—then maybe she and Nikos could become friends. Her breath hitched. If they could find their way to a friendship, maybe they could find a way to *more*.

How much more do you want?

Her heart started pounding. The air squeezed from her lungs, making her breathless.

She'd never met a man she'd wanted so *fiercely*. Sometimes she looked at him and all she could think about was making love with him. She had *important* things to think about. Siena's health, the Mabel-Constantinos feud, her father and Siena's relationship, Siena and Christian's relationship. And yet one glance at Nikos had all of that fading to nothing.

And when he stared at her with smouldering eyes that told her he felt the same...

She leaped up, fanning herself. She had to stop thinking about this. She and Nikos made no sense.

Why does it have to make sense?

If they started anything, it couldn't go anywhere.

Why does it have to go anywhere?

She was trying to form a friendship with the man, build trust.

Maybe it'll help.

'Oh, and now you really are scraping the bottom of the justification barrel.' Practically wrenching the door off its hinges, she stuck her head above deck. 'Time to put the kettle on?'

'You bet!'

She followed Nikos's voice and found him at the bow, dark hair glistening with sea spray and eyes alive with energy and satisfaction. Her mouth dried. Had he ever looked more perfect?

She cleared her throat, not entirely sure it'd work. 'You enjoyed that, didn't you? Man wrestling the elements and all that.'

His grin did the craziest things to her pulse. 'Sprung. Sorry if the ride was a bit bumpy. I hope it wasn't too harrowing.'

'Nothing disaster movie-ish about it all.' She did what she could to keep the smile on her lips and the lust from her eyes. 'It was a little anticlimactic, if the truth be told. In the best possible way,' she added in double-quick time, in case he decided they ought to bounce all the way to his grandfather's island. She wanted to be at her best when she met Vasillis Constantinos, not look like a dishevelled mouse.

'You don't look the slightest bit green.' He studied her face so intently that even from this distance she had to swallow. 'I swear, MJ, you don't have a single hair out of place.'

Was that good or bad?

'You're obviously a natural sailor.'

The warmth that flooded her almost undid her. To hide the depth of feeling his words created, she pointed at the rain clouds. 'Looks like things are about to get wet. Is there anything I can do?'

'I'm nearly done.'

She disappeared back below deck. The galley kitchen and seating area were small but well-equipped. In no time at all she had tea brewing and had cut several slices of the fruitcake she'd found among the provisions, arranged them on a plate.

The moment he clattered down the steps, the tiny cabin shrank. He collapsed onto a seat, seized a piece of cake and devoured it in two bites, before draining half a mug of tea. Without a word she topped it up, glad she'd made a large pot.

He smiled his thanks and gestured back the way he'd come. 'It's hungry work.'

Evidently. She wrapped her fingers around her mug and tried not to stare. It was as if, out here on the sea with the wind in his hair and salt on his lips, some hidden part of him had come alive.

She had to fight the urge to reach out and touch it…touch him.

He pulled out his phone. 'Let's see how long it'll take for the storm to pass.'

She watched him tap away with long, lean fingers and had a sudden vision of those fingers on her body—teasing, tantalising, exploring…giving her pleasure…

Jerking her gaze away, she seized a piece of cake and bit into it. A pointless exercise because no amount of cake could fill the ache yawning inside her.

'Looks like we could be here a while. See?'

He angled the phone towards her and she saw the storm front moving across the screen. She fingered the hem of her shirt. One leg started to jig. 'How long is a while?'

She was stranded on what suddenly felt like a tiny boat with the hottest man in the history of hot men and her hormones were acting out like a raging, seething, defiant teenager. As if that wasn't a recipe for disaster!

Lean lips pursed…

Don't think about the lips.

'It's still a good two-and-a-half hours to my grandfather's island, and it doesn't look like this storm will pass until eight o'clock.'

Eight o'clock tonight? She felt suddenly hot and then suddenly cold. Both legs started to bounce.

'There's a smaller front coming behind it too. It'll probably miss us, but...'

He trailed off. Outside, rain lashed the windows.

She forced a breath in through her nose and out through her mouth. She would *not* freak out about spending the night in a floating bathtub with Nikos. *She wouldn't.* She was an adult woman. *Be cool, MJ.* She needed to aim for unflappable. 'Looks like we're here for the night, then.' If her voice squeaked at the edges, well, who could blame it?

All the energy that had sparked him to life drained out of him. 'I'm really sorry, MJ. I should've planned all of this better.'

MJ topped up his mug with a shrug. 'You're hardly responsible for the weather, Nikos. You took the advice you were given at the marina. It sounds like this storm will have caught everyone on the hop.'

She pushed the plate holding the last piece of cake towards him and sipped her tea. Was she really as relaxed as she looked? Hadn't that kiss tied her up in knots?

He raked a hand back through his hair. He was strung tighter than a mainsail in a hurricane. Ever since he'd come below deck and found her so capably presiding over the teapot—with cake, no less—his awareness of her had grown until his entire body throbbed with it. He'd had to gulp down cake in an effort to regain a semblance of equilibrium. So far he'd only found the semblance, not the real thing.

Up on deck, when he'd been focussed on finding shelter and making sure MJ felt safe, he'd been able to push away the memory of the kiss, even as its aftermath burned in his body and lent him an energy both strange and invigorating.

Now, seated so close to her, heat and need pierced him. He couldn't look at her without wanting to haul her into his lap to kiss her again. To spend the next few hours...

Stop it!

He could do this. She didn't deserve to have him panting all over her, lusting after her. He *would* keep his wayward desires under wraps. Glancing up, he opened his mouth to say something—*anything*—but her gaze skittered away and the words, meaningless anyway, died in his throat.

Shuffling round the table, she stood and explored the small passage leading deeper into the hull. Two doors stood opposite each other and she peered into both. 'There are sleeping quarters.'

Separate sleeping quarters. 'We'll be snug as bugs,' he assured her, trying not to wince at his descent into cliché.

She hovered for a moment and then slid back into her seat, as if aware she had nowhere else to go. Outside thunder crashed and she jumped.

Rain lashed the boat. Did she feel trapped? He clenched his hands beneath the table. 'We'll be fine, MJ. I swear, you're perfectly safe.' From the elements and from him.

For a moment he could have sworn disappointment flared in her eyes, but then she blinked and they turned opaque. 'I know. I trust you.'

No Mabel had ever had reason to trust a Constantinos, or vice versa. When they'd been enemies, he'd had a script to follow. Now that they weren't, he didn't know what the hell to do. This yacht might be safely anchored, but he felt cast adrift on a vast, unknown ocean.

Unknown oceans should be terrifying. Why, then, was he filling with energy, anticipation and a mystifying sense of adventure?

'So...'

Her voice, oddly strangled, snapped him back to reality.

'This is probably where I ought to confess that I can't cook.'

He shook himself. What did that matter?

'I mean, it's hardly a fair distribution of labour, is it? You found us shelter and yet I can't even make you a meal in return.'

He leaned towards her.

Dear God, don't draw too close.

He leaned back again. 'You don't cook at all?'

'I can...uh...toss a salad.'

'How do you survive?' She didn't live in the

family home. She had her own apartment. She wouldn't have a housekeeper or cook.

Her chin lifted. 'If you work similar hours to me—and I suspect you do—then tell me, when do you find the time to cook?'

She had a point, but he sensed she was also deflecting the question. Some instinct warned him to tread carefully. He speared a leftover crumb of fruitcake and popped it in his mouth. 'I have a housekeeper. That's how I survive.'

His self-deprecation made her smile. 'There are several restaurants close to my flat who'll all make me a meal to go whenever I want. Fresh ingredients, beautifully cooked.'

'Win-win,' he agreed.

'But I don't outsource all my chores. I wash my own dishes and wipe the kitchen counters down. I even take out the rubbish.'

'So what you're saying is, if I cook, you'll clean?'

'That's *exactly* what I'm saying.'

He laughed. The jut of her chin made him to want to...

Jumping up, he slammed his knee against the top of the table. *Hell!* Rubbing it, he glanced around the kitchen, down the hallway and at his knee—anywhere but her. 'Which cabin do you want? The beds won't be made up, so I'll do them now rather than later when I won't feel like it.'

'My bag was put in that one.' She pointed to the left. 'And I'll make my own bed.'

'I don't mind.' He wanted to keep busy, keep his hands occupied with something mundane and innocuous. 'It can be tricky manoeuvring in such confined spaces, and I promise not to short-sheet your bed.'

'*I* mind.'

She didn't want him intruding on her space. Smart. It'd be wise to keep to their own dedicated areas and enforce no-go zones.

'I'm not some pampered princess you need to wait on hand and foot. If anything, *I* should be making *your* bed, as you steered us through the storm so ably.'

She smelled like every good thing a man could want—vanilla, a hint of salt and spiced rum. And she stared at him as though he was a hero. He wasn't a hero. He was a low-down, dirty creep who couldn't get thoughts of her naked body out of his mind.

'You're not making my bed, MJ.'

The words rasped out of him on a hoarse growl, and her eyes widened. She edged away. 'Okay, then. I'll just…um…go and make mine.'

She practically fled to her cabin. He stood in the middle of the galley, staring at the spot where she'd been, his hands clenching and unclenching. He *would* get a grip of himself. He would *not* lose control.

Striding into his designated cabin, he closed the door and leaned back against it. He was thirty-two years of age, for God's sake, not a horny teenager.

It took no time at all to make the bed, but he strung it out for as long as he could. Eventually, though, manners forced him to move. She was his guest. Glancing at the rain-slicked glass of the porthole, he shoved down a sigh. If only the damn rain would stop, they could sit out on deck, maybe even eat out there.

On deck, with all the sea before them and all the sky above them, they wouldn't feel so confined. He might be able to focus on something other than MJ's lips, or burying his face in her neck to inhale her scent, or imagining what she'd look like lying abandoned beneath him.

Don't think about that.

He shot out of his cabin. MJ shot from hers at the same time, with much the same haste, and they crashed into each other. He grabbed her upper arms to stop her careening back and colliding with the wall.

'Sorry, I…'

She glanced up and her words stuttered to a halt. She moistened her lips and he could have groaned out loud when her gaze lowered to his mouth with a hunger that sent sparks firing through him.

'Why did you kiss me before—up on deck?'

He fought to draw air into cramped lungs. 'It seemed like a good idea at the time.'

'Did it? I wonder why?' Her brows drew together and she almost glared. 'I haven't been able to stop thinking about it.' Her hands slammed to her hips. 'You don't strike me as the kind of man who goes around kissing strange women on a whim.'

'I don't think you're strange, MJ.' She felt like a... Damn it, she felt like a friend, a kindred spirit! 'And it wasn't a whim. I haven't been able to get the thought of kissing you out of my head since...'

'Since my hotel room in Geneva.'

'Since the moment you walked into my office five days ago.'

Her throat bobbed and her eyes grew huge. 'It's madness.'

'Total,' he agreed.

'I'm not even sure you like me.'

The vulnerability shining in those eyes nearly gutted him. His hands slipped up to curve around her shoulders. 'You sure about that?'

'You're still afraid to trust me.'

It was true, but only sort of. 'Not because I don't trust you, MJ, but because I don't trust myself. I know what I owe my family.' And yet, staring into those green eyes that promised refuge, hope and a safe haven, all his reservations dissolved to nothing.

'So...' Her breath hitched. 'You're saying you think I'm a nice person and that...that maybe you like me.'

'That's exactly what I'm saying.' He gave a single hard nod. 'But I can't make you any promises, and you deserve more than that.' A woman like Marjorie Joan Mabel deserved the very best a man had to offer. She deserved *all* of a man's allegiance, not merely a fraction of it.

She reached up and touched his face. 'You say it as if it means nothing when it means everything.'

A loud crack of thunder sounded overhead and she gave a low laugh. 'I once likened our families to a Shakespearean play.'

She'd meant *Romeo and Juliet*, with its tragic, star-crossed lovers.

'But personally, I've always been more partial to *The Tempest*.'

And then she stood on tiptoe and kissed him.

MJ hadn't meant to kiss Nikos.

Correction. She hadn't *planned* to kiss him. But, when they'd barrelled into each other coming out of their rooms at exactly the same time... Well, it had felt a lot like fate.

It wasn't just that he set her pulse on fire. Though he did.

It wasn't just that she could see in his eyes that

he wanted her every bit as much as she did him. Though she did.

And *that* was headier than vintage champagne.

It was because he held himself on too tight a leash—a leash called duty and responsibility. He didn't want his actions to cause pain to anyone—not to his family, and not to her.

Because he finally saw her. The real her.

It was frightening and exhilarating in equal measure. He'd had the courage to look past first impressions and their families' prejudice and history. While he initially might have wanted to believe her to be a treacherous Mabel, playing some deep game to gain an advantage, he'd ultimately judged her...justly.

Despite the volatility of their initial meeting, he'd treated her with courtesy. He hadn't mocked her fear of dogs or exploited it. He hadn't bad-mouthed her great-aunt or father to her face. He'd remained true to their deal. Nikos Constantinos was a man of honour and he made her feel cared for, protected and safe. He made her feel smart and beautiful. He made her feel cherished.

She wanted to make him forget duty and responsibility for a little while, to give him a holiday from it. And she also wanted to make him feel beautiful and cherished.

That was why she'd kissed him.

But the moment their lips met, all rational thought fled. Sensation flooded her as his lips opened to hers and he kissed her back with what felt like all of himself. All MJ could do was wrap her arms around his shoulders and hold on.

One large hand cradled her head and the other splayed across her hip. Tongues met in an erotic dance, teeth nipped playfully as he backed her against the wall behind and they moved against each other until it wasn't possible to get any closer while fully clothed.

Fierce need and heat pummelled her. She hooked a leg around his waist and he held it in place, his hand splayed across her buttock, fingers digging into her flesh with an urgency that made her tremble. He pressed against her more intimately exactly where she wanted.

She moaned his name, low and needy.

He stilled, resting his forehead on the wall beside her head, but the quivering of his muscles told her how much discipline it took.

'MJ, if you want me to stop…'

Her answer was to reach down and open the door to her cabin and they fell inwards. Only his strength and balance stopped them from tumbling to the floor. Not that there was enough floor space for them to fall to. But the bed was plenty big enough for two.

'Don't you dare stop, Nikos. I want this. I want you.' And then she kissed him—with passion and urgency, unable to hide just how much she wanted him.

She didn't want to stop. She didn't want to think. All she wanted to do was feel.

A low growl rumbled from his throat, thrilling her every nerve ending. He took charge of the kiss, cradling her face, angling it and holding it still so she couldn't move. Then he laved every millimetre of her lips with attention until her fingernails dug into his arms and her body arched into his, silently begging for his attention.

Tearing the shirt from the hem of his trousers, she explored the smooth skin of his back and the bumps of his spine, before dancing her fingers down and around to his abdomen. He sucked in a breath that made something inside of her sing. With more eagerness than grace, she hauled his shirt over his head, and her breath caught as she stared at him. 'You're beautiful, Nikos.'

She reached for the waistband of his boxers, but he batted her fingers away, lifted the hem of her shirt and pulled it gently over her head. With a flick of his fingers, he released the catch on her bra and drew it down her arms.

His gaze darkened and he reached out to caress her breasts, his thumbs grazing her nipples. Her quick intake of breath sounded through the cabin and she arched into his touch, unashamedly wanton. With someone else she might have felt self-conscious, but Nikos gazed at her with such open approval she felt she could do no wrong—

not here, not now, not in the privacy of this haven they'd created for themselves.

Her capri pants and knickers followed the rest of her clothing, but he again dodged her fingers as they reached for the waistband of his boxers. 'I'm keeping these on for the moment.'

'But—'

'I'm going to explore every inch of your body, MJ. I'm planning on giving you the most mind-blowing orgasm of your life, and I don't want to be distracted. But, once I've done that, *then* I'm going to get naked and do it all over again.'

Her breath jammed at his words. Her pulse went ballistic at the hunger flaring in his eyes. He laid her on the bed and tears pricked the backs of her eyes at his tenderness. And then he proceeded to show her exactly what he'd meant.

His hands and mouth moved over every inch of her, exploring, worshipping…making her gasp and arch into his touch as he built and fanned an inferno inside her. It burned, raged and demanded until she could no longer think, only feel. She urged, begged and pleaded for him to go faster, but he refused to rush. It was as if he was taking as much relish in her building pleasure as she was. She gave herself over to it until finally she found herself flung into a vortex of sensual delight greater than any she'd ever experienced. Sensation sparked along every nerve ending, the reverberations reaching every part of her body.

She floated back to earth to find herself cradled in Nikos's arms. When she'd caught her breath and could make her limbs work, she lifted up on one elbow to stare down at him. 'That was incredible.'

He laughed, gently pushing a strand of hair behind her ear. 'If you keep looking at me like that, Marjorie, you're going to give me a swollen head.'

'You deserve a swollen head.'

But there was something more than his ego on her mind. Reaching down, she palmed him through his boxers. The hard length of him pulsed against her hand and he sucked in a breath. A tic started at the centre of her, and her body tightened again, hungry for him once more.

'Can we now dispense with the rest of your clothes?' She'd wanted to make her voice playful, but it came out breathless, impatient...needy.

'MJ?'

'I want to see you naked,' she whispered, meeting his gaze.

Without a word, he rose and shucked off the rest of his clothes. And then swore. 'I'll be right back. I...'

She held up a hand to stay him. She'd been in the process of rising to her knees to study him better, but she diverted to the bedside table and plucked a box of condoms from her handbag.

A slow grin spread across his face. 'You're my kind of woman, MJ. You know that?'

She didn't answer, except to pull him back down beside her to press kisses along his chest and explore his magnificent body as thoroughly as he had hers.

All too soon, though, he'd rolled her over, his clever fingers and mouth making her breathy and needy all over again. 'Please, Nikos, please,' she found herself begging.

Covering her body with his, he brushed her hair from her eyes. Her gaze found his and he joined their two bodies in a single fluid stroke.

She gasped at the spine-tingling pressure, at the sense of fullness and completeness...at the perfection. Neither of them moved or breathed for several long seconds.

Wonder that was no doubt echoed in her face spread across his. And then they were moving in unison and it didn't feel as if they were merely touching each other's bodies, but something deeper and more important, more essential. Before she could work out what it was, sensation and pleasure fogged her mind and took her over completely. Their cries mingled as they found release and rapture together.

Nikos didn't know how long he lay there, stunned at the intensity of making love with MJ, relishing the afterglow and the feeling of her wrapped against his side. She didn't speak, but her fingers trailed an idle path across his chest, as did his on her back. He had a feeling she was as shocked and awed as him.

Making love with her had felt like making the world right when he hadn't realised it was wrong. It was as if something inside her counterbalanced something inside him. When their bodies had been joined, she'd felt essential to...

He frowned. To what? His happiness? His success? His life? It was too much too soon, and he had no idea how to temper any of it.

Or how to re-establish the boundaries they'd smashed when they'd given into temptation.

A weight bore down on him. Where on earth did he think this thing between them could lead?

'I'm getting the distinct impression you've started over-thinking things.'

Her soft admonishment shouldn't have surprised him. She was so attuned to him it should scare him. He turned his head to meet her gaze. 'I would hate you to regret what just happened.'

'I don't regret it.' Small white teeth worried her bottom lip. 'It was more intense than I expected.'

He nodded, went to say something and then hesitated.

'Go on,' she urged. 'What were you going to say?'

His lips settled into a grim line. 'I can't help feeling we're going to have to pay the piper for scaling such heights, MJ.'

She reached up and touched his face. 'Maybe

we will. And maybe the price will be worth paying. Nikos, neither one of us knows what the future holds. But we won't have to pay up just yet. It's only late afternoon—we have the rest of the night and tomorrow morning before the world intrudes on us again. I vote we relish it while we can.'

How could any man resist this woman? He pressed a quick kiss to those eminently kissable lips. 'In which case, we need to keep our strength up. Hungry?'

Her smile filled his soul. 'Ravenous.'

CHAPTER NINE

NIKOS MADE A simple meal of stir-fried vegetables and noodles that they devoured. And then they made love again. And, when they woke in the wee small hours, they turned to each other and made love once more with a dreamy kind of reverence that almost undid her. They fell asleep in each other's arms and woke to a still, cloud-free morning.

On deck, sipping coffee in their tiny sheltered cove, it felt as if they were the only people in the world.

Nikos sent her a smile that heated her from the inside out. 'Ever been skinny-dipping?'

She choked on her coffee. 'It's daylight!'

He gave a lazy shrug. 'Who's to see us? We're all alone out here, MJ. You, me and this perfect sea.'

Standing, he lifted his shirt over his head and tossed it to the deck, his eyes sending her a sensual challenge as he pushed his shorts down his hips. He stood in front of her, completely naked and her mouth dried. Dear Lord, the man was magnificent.

'Chicken?' he taunted with another devilish grin.

She'd have shot back a sassy retort, but he chose that moment to turn and walk to the rear of the yacht, and the words dried in her throat as she took in broad shoulders, lean hips and taut buttocks. She leaned forward with a frown. There were marks...

Heat scorched her cheeks. The marks on Nikos's buttocks had been made by her *fingernails*. In the throes of passion when he'd sent her hurtling over the edge...again and again; when she'd held him as close to her as she physically could.

She blinked when both his feet left the deck and he arced through the air, barely making a splash as he executed a perfect dive. She raced across to peer over the side and held her breath. His head broke the water a short way away. The grin he sent her as he shook water from his eyes was pure sin and playfulness. 'Come on in, the water's fine.'

She bit her lip. 'I've never skinny-dipped before.'

'Then you haven't lived.'

She glanced around. Not another boat was in sight. And a completely relaxed, grinning Nikos was impossible to resist. Shucking off her clothes, she jumped in the water and resurfaced with a gasp. 'It's freezing!'

In two strokes Nikos was in front of her and his arms slid about her waist. 'Maybe I can warm you up.' His teeth tugged gently on her ear, making her boneless. And then he dunked her.

She bobbed up a moment later, laughing. They

swam and cavorted like children for a glorious half-hour before climbing back on board to dry each other off. Where, of course, they became distracted again, before finally indulging in a hearty breakfast.

They'd planned to set off for Vasillios's island immediately after they'd eaten, but Nikos saw her gazing at the tiny island and he nodded. 'It'd be fun to explore.'

The man could apparently read her mind now.

He shrugged, a roguish twinkle lighting his eyes. 'It wouldn't make much difference if we set off after lunch instead.' Sobering, he reached out to touch her cheek. 'I can't seem to get enough of you at the moment, Marjorie. I want to hold on to this moment for as long as I can.'

Her heart thundered when he pulled her in for a kiss. She felt exactly the same. Taking a moment to catch her breath, she gestured to the island. 'Will we swim to it?' No matter what Nikos said, she wasn't walking around that island naked.

He laughed as if he'd read that thought in her face. 'We'll use the dingy and row across. We'll need our shoes.'

His powerful arms and shoulders made short work of the journey. Hand in hand, they explored the pebbly beach and then trekked up the rocky rise. She hesitated before they could crest it.

He sent her one of those grins that could turn

her insides to warm marshmallow. 'Worried we might bump into someone?'

'Of course not.' The island was deserted except for seabirds and the occasional small lizard. It was just…once they crested the hill, they'd see the rest of the world again, and it would start to intrude. Everything inside her protested at the thought.

She turned away with a frown, pretending to admire the view of the beach below and the yacht at anchor. Her heart protested it far too vehemently, and that couldn't be good. They hadn't planned this to happen, and they'd not made any promises.

It'd be crazy for either one of them to invest too much in what had happened here in this gorgeous place, and yet it felt crazy not to. She had no notion of what the rules were for such a situation, though. They were going to have to make them up as they went along, which was going to be interesting, when she suspected he was as befuddled by all this as she was.

Damn it. That kind of 'go with the flow' attitude was more Siena's province than hers. She liked forward planning and knowing what to expect.

What to expect?

A hollow laugh sounded through her and her heart dropped to the soles of her feet. What on earth was she thinking? This thing between her and Nikos…it was fleeting. It was always going to be fleeting.

Still, did it have to be *this* fleeting?

'MJ?'

She turned back and made herself smile, reached up and took the hand he offered. 'Just catching my breath.' She gestured back the way they'd come. 'It's beautiful here.'

Another half a dozen steps brought them to a meadow of golden grass dotted all over with blue and white wildflowers. She laughed when she realised the meadow was ringed on three sides by a rock cliff. They were still cocooned in their own little world and it felt like an omen. A good omen.

Rosemary scented the air and, with the sun warm on her arms, MJ felt as if they'd stumbled on Eden. She squeezed his hand. 'What a perfect place for a picnic.'

'What a perfect place to pitch a tent.'

'On a clear night the stars must be amazing here.'

They strolled around the perimeter, found a small spring to drink from and then sat on a large, flat rock, MJ seated between Nikos's thighs and resting back against his chest, his arms circling her shoulders. 'What an utterly idyllic morning,' she murmured. 'I've never been more grateful for a storm in my life.'

He pressed a kiss to her temple. 'I'll second that.'

Questions bombarded her. Would they ever make love again once they left this place? How did Nikos want them to act around his grandfather? Did he want to keep what had happened here a secret? When all this was over, would he want to see her again? She didn't ask a single one, refusing to break the spell. There'd be time enough to ask them once they'd set sail.

Not that she had any intention of asking that last question. He'd make it clear if he wanted to see her again.

A sigh whispered from her. 'I guess there aren't any more storms forecast for this afternoon?'

His arms tightened about her fractionally. 'Afraid not.'

Had he checked?

Of course he'd checked. As their skipper, it was his job to know the weather forecast. It'd be foolish to read too much into it.

They sat there for as long as they could, silently soaking each other in—at least, that was what it felt like. As if they needed it to shore themselves up for what was to come. Eventually, by mutual consent, they silently rose and made their way back down to the beach, holding hands when they could.

While Nikos busied himself readying the dingy, MJ bent down to collect a pink-hued pebble washed smooth by the tide. She slipped it into the pocket of her shorts. A memento. A talisman. Her fingers closed around it—a good luck charm.

For lunch they ate a salad of tomato, cucumber, red onion, olives and feta cheese in a delicious dressing that Nikos made. She wiped her bowl clean with pitta bread, shaking her head when he offered her more. 'That was delicious. Compliments to the chef. You're an excellent cook, Nikos.'

Her words made him chuckle. 'I threw together a salad, MJ, not a three-course meal.'

'You made that dressing—which was exquisite, I might add.'

He set his plate aside and eyed her over the rim of his glass of sparkling water. 'Why do I get the impression there's more to your "no cooking" story than you're letting on?'

The question was asked gently and she knew that if she brushed it away he'd let the matter drop. But they'd shared so much, and it felt right to tell him something she'd never revealed to another soul. 'It's a bit silly,' she said, biting the inside of her cheek.

'I doubt that.'

His gaze never left hers but she found she couldn't look at him as she told the story. She stared down at her feet instead, fiddling with the laces on her tennis shoes. 'When I was nine, I developed a real bee in my bonnet about learning how to cook. Siena's thing at that time was painting. My mother arranged for Siena to attend art classes two afternoons a week and promised me that, on those afternoons, she'd teach me how to cook.'

'What happened?' he asked when she halted.

The gentleness in his voice had tears prickling the backs of her eyes. Because, yes, something had obviously gone wrong or she'd have been quite happy and capable of whipping up a meal for ten.

'We had three lessons, and I can't tell you how much I loved them.' And then had come that angry phone call that had had her mother slamming down the phone and directing Alice, their housekeeper, to finish the lesson.

'And?'

'My mother was called away before our cake had finished cooking. I never saw her alive again.'

His quick intake of breath speared into the centre of her. 'Oh, sweetheart.' He reached out and gripped her hands, and his endearment gave her the courage to lift her head. 'You don't cook because it reminds you of your mother and makes you miss her more.'

His understanding shouldn't have surprised her. 'I told you it was silly. She wouldn't want me to not cook because of her, but whenever I've tried I just... I get sad.'

His eyes darkened and the corners of his mouth

turned down. 'I'm sorry you lost your mother, MJ.'

'It's not your fault she's gone, Nikos.' It was the fault of that angry voice on the phone. 'It's crazy, isn't it? She's been gone for nearly twenty years and yet I still miss her every single day.'

The moment the words left her mouth, the jangling of ropes and snapping of sails off to their right had them swinging to stare as a large yacht journeyed past, so close she could make out the people on board.

They waved. She and Nikos waved back, and watched silently as it rounded the far end of the island and disappeared from view. But the image of it remained like an aftershock.

She glanced back at Nikos and winced at the lines bracketing his mouth. 'And so the real world finally intrudes,' she murmured, her heart sinking.

'Yes.'

The single word was blunt, uncompromising, and answered more of her earlier questions than she wanted it to. Her chest grew heavy, and for some ridiculous reason her eyes started to burn. 'I'm guessing that what's happened here isn't something you want to share with your grandfather.'

He hesitated.

'Don't worry, Nikos. I understand.' She'd be his dirty little secret.

He swore. 'I'm starting to think this wasn't a good idea.'

Her head rocked back, but before she could form a lucid response he said, 'I'm not talking about what's happened here over the last twenty-four hours!'

The sharpness of his tone reassured her. She searched his face then let out a slow breath. 'Good.' Because as far as she was concerned the last twenty-four hours hadn't just been a revelation, they'd been a gift she'd treasure forever.

'I'm talking about taking you to my grandfather's island. My grandfather...'

She watched him struggle to find the words to describe Vasillios without making him sound like an ogre. She took pity on him. 'Your grandfather hates anyone with the same surname as mine.'

He neither confirmed nor denied it, but he didn't have to. 'I don't want his attitude to hurt you.'

'I don't want his attitude to hurt you either.' Her words made him blink and she shrugged. 'It'll take too much time to return me to the mainland now. Besides, I feel we're set on this path, don't you? It feels too late to turn back.'

He raked a hand through his hair, indecision rife in his eyes.

She reached out and touched his arm. 'I didn't ask you to shield me from anything, Nikos. I'm a big girl and I can look after myself. I'll hold my own against your grandfather—you'll see.'

She gestured to their yacht. 'Come on. Haul anchor or cast off, or whatever the lingo is, while I go and clean up the lunch things.'

Three hours later, on a spectacularly beautiful Greek island, MJ and Nikos entered Vasillios's beautiful but remote villa. She glanced around the interior, taking in the general splendour. While Vasillios might have shut himself away from the world, he'd not forgone his creature comforts.

She turned to Nikos. 'So your grandfather is a modern day Mr Havisham, sitting around in the last suit he ever wore when courting my great-aunt and nursing his heartbreak and bitterness?'

'Not quite,' a wry voice said from the staircase behind her.

She closed her eyes and grimaced before turning round. 'Mr Constantinos Senior, I presume? You weren't supposed to hear that.'

He moved to stand in front of her, but didn't proffer his hand. 'And you're one of the Ms Mabels.'

'Marjorie Joan, otherwise known as MJ.' She held her breath. She wanted this man to like her and the realisation shocked her. Did she want that because of her great-aunt or because of Nikos?

'You look like her,' he finally said.

'So few people see the resemblance.'

'You have the same mouth.'

Her lips twitched. 'Are you referring to its shape or what comes out of it?'

Dark eyes twinkled briefly. 'I'm a gentleman. Of course I meant the shape.'

His words made her laugh. 'I knew I'd like you. Even though your stupidity, stiff-necked pride and pig-headed stubbornness broke my great-aunt's heart...not to mention your own.'

Vasillios's head reared back. Nikos gaped at her. 'You can't talk to my grandfather like that!'

She shot him an apologetic grimace. 'Ordinarily, I'd agree with you. As a rule, I think the older generation should be treated with respect. But that doesn't give them a free pass.' She wrinkled her nose. 'If it makes you feel any better, I accused my great-aunt of exactly the same things. The pair of them were both utter idiots.'

Nikos stared, as MJ strode across to the backpack she'd refused to hand over to his grandfather's staff, and pinched the bridge of his nose. Bringing her here had been a *bad* idea.

'What is the meaning of this, Nikos?' Any amusement his grandfather might have harboured had disappeared. 'Why would you bring a Mabel—' he spat the name out as if it tasted bad in his mouth '—here to my island, my haven... my refuge?'

MJ came back, a package clasped in her hands,

and Nikos could have groaned out loud at the way her lips twitched. 'You live in splendour here, sir, so I refuse to feel sorry for you.'

She was a force of nature and he had no idea how to stop her.

'Your grandson had no choice because I blackmailed him.'

His grandfather's face darkened. Nikos didn't know whether to laugh or cry, whether to try and wrest control of the situation or to let things run their course.

'But you're going to need to offer us refreshments before we embark on that particular story. In the meantime, I have something for you. If you have the courage to read it.'

She held up the parcel and his grandfather's eyes flashed. 'I am no coward.'

The laugh she gave made Nikos wince. 'Excuse me for contradicting you, but rather than trying to win back the woman you supposedly loved you focused instead on trying to win back a trinket you'd given her.' She shook her head. 'That doesn't sound like the actions of a brave man to me.'

'The Ananke necklace is no mere trinket!' his grandfather roared. 'It's an heirloom worth millions!'

Her quick intake of breath and the small step she took away from Vasillios made Nikos ache. A burn started up in his chest.

'Did the necklace matter more to you than my great-aunt's heart?' she whispered.

She held the parcel to her chest and stroked a hand over it, as if to give it—or herself—comfort. The expression on her face—a mix of sadness, vulnerability and loneliness—had Nikos wanting to drag her into his arms and give her whatever comfort he could.

Just as he'd wanted to when she'd spoken of her mother earlier. He bit back an expletive. This was why he needed to stay the hell away from her, and why he should never, *never* have let things between them become so explosively intimate! If MJ found out the truth, she'd hold his family responsible for the death of her mother.

His heart clenched. What was more, he wouldn't blame her.

'I spent a lot of time with my great-aunt in her final months. She knew she was dying and had time to prepare. We often talked about you and the Ananke necklace, Mr Constantinos. You accused her of cheating on you, but she never did. She remained true to you until the day she died. She left both the necklace and this diary to me— to do with as I thought best. She knew I had hopes that fences could be mended between our two families.'

Nikos's heart beat harder. He wanted to mend those fences too. Between them, could he and MJ make that happen?

'I think you ought to read her diary—to see for yourself and understand the heart of the woman you spent most of your adult life battling.'

The older man pointed a shaking finger. 'If what you say is true, why did she never tell me this herself?'

'You got married.'

Vasillios abruptly turned and strode to the window.

'She thought you'd forgotten about her, that she'd read more into your love affair than she should have. Of course, your marriage ended badly, and you blamed her for it. But she merely considered herself a convenient scapegoat so you could cast yourself in the role of tragic hero and exile yourself from the world.'

Vasillios swung round, his face darkening. 'You know nothing of these events!'

Her face softened, as if she empathised with the older man, and Nikos had to brace his hands on his knees. MJ was caught up in events she didn't fully understand, events that had the ability not only to hurt her but to crush her.

He struggled to get air into suddenly cramped lungs. He had to prevent that from happening.

'I know. I'm merely narrating how my great-aunt interpreted events. Unfortunately, she had her pride too, of which you're undoubtedly well aware. She was every bit as stubborn as you. Why on earth should she be the one to make the first move…blah-blah-blah?' She shook her head. 'But, as I told her often enough, stubborn pride won't keep you warm at night.'

The heightened colour faded from the older man's face. He gestured at the package MJ held. 'You want to give the diary to me? You want me to read it?'

'Yes.'

'Why?'

'Because she loved you. And I think you loved her. Reading her diary will prove that to you and I think it will bring you peace. And, Mr Constantinos, that's all I want for our two families—peace.'

His grandfather's eyes flashed. 'There will be no peace until the Ananke necklace is once again in the hands of the Constantinos family. I notice you do not offer *that* to me.'

'With the greatest respect, sir, my generation may have very different thoughts on the matter.'

'What do you plan to do with it?'

She glanced at Nikos briefly and everything inside him drew tight. 'It's a valuable art deco necklace designed by a celebrated artist who died before his time, which makes it rare. I think the best place for it is the Victoria and Albert Museum.'

'Over my dead body!' Vasillios roared.

She gave an involuntary laugh and Nikos knew she was thinking of that moment in his office when he'd said those exact same words to her.

'You mock me?' he roared, his white hair vibrating with outrage.

'No, I don't, but you're impossible.' She said it as if speaking to a recalcitrant child, and he had a feeling she did so deliberately to enrage the older man further.

'You should not have come here, Ms Mabel. You know our history. What if you were to meet with…an accident?'

Before Nikos could intervene, she laughed again. 'You and your grandson have much in common, but I'm not afraid of either of you. You can both be fiery and passionate, and no doubt cold and calculating too…and, yes, you both hate my family.'

Her words rang in Nikos's ears and shame pooled in his gut. He wanted to fall down into the nearest chair and cover his eyes, avert his gaze…try to un-hear her words.

'But neither of you would ever physically harm a woman. And, if you did actually manage to frighten me, the shame of it would burn in your soul far longer than my fear would last.'

The older man's eyes dropped. He took a step away before glancing at Nikos. 'See that Ms Mabel is shown to one of the guest rooms and then join me in the library.' Without another word, he turned and strode away.

MJ watched him go. Blowing out a breath, she turned to Nikos with a shrug. 'I think he likes me.'

Her deadpan delivery had him fighting an entirely inappropriate laugh. 'You didn't think to clue me in about—' he gestured to her and then to where his grandfather had been standing '—that?'

'That had nothing to do with you, Nikos. Or me. It had everything to do with him and her.'

'You didn't tell me because you don't trust me.' The words left a bad taste on his tongue.

She took a step closer and stared up into his face, those green eyes intent. 'Should I trust you?'

He wanted to roar that of course she could trust him. But he couldn't. Not when he was keeping from her a vital piece of the puzzle surrounding their families

You're not keeping it out of spite or to hurt her.

And yet it still left him feeling as if he had a stain on his soul.

'Are you going to tell him about the deal we made?'

Her question made him blink. 'That if I help you find Siena you'll give me the Ananke necklace?' He rolled his shoulders. 'He's my grandfather, MJ. All his life he's loved and cared for me. He saved my mother's life once. I'm not going to keep secrets from him.'

She touched a finger to her lips in a pose of exaggerated deep thought. 'So does that mean you're also planning to tell him what happened last night when we were stranded by the storm?'

Hell, no!

She laughed softly. 'So you pick and choose your secrets, then?'

He had no response for that because it was exactly what he was doing. Without another word he led her upstairs to the best of the guest rooms.

She barely glanced around. 'How long do you think we'll be here?'

'Only overnight.' He suspected the less time she and his grandfather spent together, the better. He turned to leave, halted and turned back. 'While we're here, MJ...' *Damn it. The words shouldn't be so hard to get out.* 'I mean tonight...'

She glanced up, waited for him to continue and then nodded, as if realising what he was trying to say. 'You won't be visiting my room and you'd prefer it if I didn't make any midnight forays to yours.'

A light in the back of her eyes went out, and he felt like an utter heel. But she straightened, both hands clasped at her waist. 'Nikos, let me make this easy on the both of us. What happened last night and this morning was lovely, and to be cherished. But we both know it was a moment out of time.'

Was she calling a halt to this thing between them?

Everything inside him roared a protest.

'It can't happen again, unless...'

He found himself leaning towards her. 'Unless what?'

She met his gaze squarely. 'Unless we're both prepared to take the next step.'

His mouth dried. He wanted to. He wanted to take that next step with an intensity that made his hands tremble. But she knew how things stood between their families. How could they ever make things work?

He pressed thumbs and forefingers to his eyes. How could he contemplate hurting his father and grandfather like that?

He pulled his hands away, darkness gathering beneath his breastbone. Even if they could overcome his father's and his grandfather's objections, and her father's... Even if by some miracle they could reconcile them to it...

His heart started to thud. He'd need to tell her what had happened between their parents. Nobody but his father and him knew the full story. And Nikos had promised never to tell.

He would have to break his word. Or ask his father to release him from that promise.

His heart thumped harder. There might be a way...

'MJ, I know that in an ideal world you want the necklace donated to a museum, but just think for a moment. If having the necklace would bring my grandfather peace and end our families' hostilities, then isn't that a great outcome? After all, that's the goal you're really after.'

'But it *wouldn't* end it, would it? Your father and grandfather would be happy, but my father wouldn't.'

It was true... 'You and I don't have to buy into any of that nonsense, though.'

'Until a week ago you *had* been buying into that nonsense. And now you want me to believe that you don't?'

'I can't believe I'm saying this.' He reached out and took both of her hands, gripping them tightly. 'You've forced me to see things differently, and I like your way of seeing things. I...' he hesitated over the word but held her gaze nonetheless. '*Love* what you're trying to achieve.'

Her mouth fell open.

It was almost a declaration—he was aware of that. But she was so fearless and he suddenly wanted to be brave too. Brave for her. 'We might not be able to achieve the ultimate ideal outcome, but we can temper the situation, improve it. Isn't that enough? Especially if it also means Christian and Siena can be together?'

She pulled her hands from his and raked them back through her hair.

'I don't want to say goodbye to you, MJ. I want to explore what we have. I think it's special.'

'I want that too.'

'With the necklace, I can reconcile my family to all of those things.'

But she didn't throw herself into his arms. Instead her eyes filled. 'The only way to end our families' feud is to get rid of the thing that's been at the heart of all the trouble—the Ananke necklace. As long as it lies between us, there won't be peace, Nikos. There'll always be the perception that one family or the other has the upper hand. It'll continue to breed hate and resentment, no matter how hard we try to mediate that.'

'But—'

'I will *not* bequeath that legacy to my children.'

A burn started up at the centre of him.

'People who value things higher than people will never find happiness, and they won't find peace. I want nothing to do with the necklace, Nikos. It's a curse, and I refuse to have it as part of my life.'

CHAPTER TEN

MJ SHOWERED. SHE felt dirty, tainted, but it wasn't the kind of taint that hot water and soap could wash away.

She'd hurt Nikos.

She hadn't meant to, but it didn't change the fact that she had. It didn't mean she wasn't breaking her own heart as well. Covering her face with her hands, she forced herself to breathe through the weight settling on her chest.

Stop moping. She needed to move, needed to try and dispel some of the agitation that had her in its grip.

Slipping down the stairs, she let herself out of the back door and deliberately strode away from Vasillios's mansion. She didn't want to run into the older man again. Not while he was in a temper. And she had no appetite for accidentally overhearing a conversation between he and his grandson.

Her hands clenched. She could imagine the older man's *triumph* when Nikos told him about the deal she'd made with him. Vasillios had broken her great-aunt's heart. Why should he get everything he wanted now?

Planting herself on a boulder, she glared at the spectacular view of blue sea filtered through the grey-green leaves of olive trees that marched down the slope to a rocky headland. After a moment, she huffed out a laugh. Closing her eyes, she focused on her breathing, on draining the negative emotions from her mind.

One thing the older generations had unwittingly taught her was that, in holding on to such negative emotions, the only person she'd truly hurt would be herself. She might have no say in what was done with the Ananake necklace once she gave it to Nikos—*if* he found Siena—but she could at least break that cycle of bitterness in her own life.

Eventually she started to breathe more easily. Vasillios hadn't got everything he wanted—he'd lost the love of his life through his own actions. And Aunt Joan hadn't been blameless either. She could have ended Vasillios's animosity at any point. They'd both chosen their pride over declaring their real feelings.

Aren't you in danger of doing the same?

She rubbed a hand across her chest, but couldn't shift the ache beneath her breastbone. She concentrated on getting one good breath into cramped lungs and then very slowly shook her head.

Nikos might be able to reconcile his father and grandfather to Christian's and Siena's relationship if the Ananke necklace was once again in the Constantinos fold, but he'd never gain her father's acceptance of the situation. Not on those terms. Which meant her greatest fear would be realised—her father and Siena would become estranged—and the thought broke her heart.

Even if by some miracle an uneasy truce was brokered, the peace between the two families would always be fragile. For as long as the Ananke necklace remained in one or the other's possession, fighting could break out again at a moment's notice. She dropped her head to her hands. She wanted no part of that.

Not even for the man you love?

Very slowly her head came up. She stared at the horizon. In her peripheral vision she saw birds twitching in the trees, fluttering from branch to branch, but inside her everything had stilled. She *loved* Nikos.

Of course she did. It made perfect sense. After their initial rocky start, they'd worked together as a team. He'd kept his word and hadn't tried to shake her off or lose her. For heaven's sake, he'd even brought her here to his grandfather's island. Nikos was honourable to the core. And reasonable—he'd listened to her side of things and had seen the justice of what she wanted to achieve, even as he remained sceptical that she could pull it off.

He hadn't tried to take advantage of her fear of dogs—he hadn't belittled her or made her feel less. Instead he'd been kind and understanding, and had done everything to help her feel safe and secure. *Of course* she loved him.

She glanced skywards, kinking an eyebrow. 'And I'm in Greece, so of course the gods are laughing at me.'

I want to explore what we have.

Nikos's earlier words played through her mind and her eyes filled. So did she. But for that to happen would mean him choosing her over the necklace. *That* was a contest she had no hope of winning.

Footsteps sounded in the undergrowth and she hastily dashed the tears away before swinging round. Nikos strode towards her, his eyes turbulent and his mouth set in a hard, straight line. Her heart thundered and she had to wrap her arms around her knees to stop from leaping to her feet and throwing herself at him.

'I saw you walk this way from the library window.' He gestured at the boulder. 'May I?'

She shuffled over and he thumped down beside her. It was clear things hadn't gone well with his grandfather. Not that she could ask him about it.

Citrus and sandalwood filled her senses. She breathed it in and held it close for a moment, before breathing out again. 'I'm sorry I was so hard on your grandfather, Nikos. I should've been gentler, kinder.'

'He should've been more reasonable. But when it comes to the past and your great-aunt he has no reason or rationality.' He placed the diary in her lap. 'He refuses to read it—said it'd be full of lies—and told me to give it back to you.'

She ran a hand over the cover. 'Well…at least I tried.'

'I shouldn't have brought you here. I'm sorry. I'd hoped that meeting you would soften him, give him a different view of things, but I miscalculated the strength of…'

She aimed for levity. 'My charm?'

His lips twitched but settled back into a straight line a moment later. 'His stubbornness.'

'He's had fifty years to brood on his sense of injury. That sort of thing can't be overcome overnight.' She stared at the diary. 'I'm sorry he won't read this, though. I thought it might bring him peace, but…'

'But?'

The way he stared at her made her feel like a goddess. She dragged her gaze back to the horizon and tried to control the racing of her pulse. 'Can you imagine how confronting it would be to discover that what you'd thought was true—and was the reason for all of your life's decisions—had been a lie?'

'The regret would kill him, not bring him peace.'

She opened the diary to the final pages and read aloud.

'"*Vasilli, if you ever read this, I want you to know that I loved you to the end of my days. Not a single day passes that I don't think of you, that I don't wish you were here by my side. Not a single day passes that I don't wish I'd answered you differently when you accused me of being unfaithful to you all those years ago.*

"'But how could I have been unfaithful when I never saw any man except you? I thought you knew that. In my pride and my hurt, I thought you should've known that. I wanted you to fight for me. When you didn't, I thought you no longer cared. And then you married so soon after...

"'I kept the necklace so you wouldn't forget me. I couldn't bear the thought of you giving it to another woman. If I'm honest, I thought you would come after me, and that once we were face-to-face again we would be able to patch things up. By the time I realised that was never going to happen, too much time had passed and it felt as if our fates were sealed. We should've fought harder for one another, my love. We were a pair of fools. But I want you to know that in my dreams I have danced with you every night for the last fifty years.

"'Adieu, my dear Vasilli, from your ever devoted Joanie.'"

Nikos dragged a hand down his face and swore softly.

She closed the diary. 'The regrets would be great, but wouldn't those words gladden his heart?'

'Only if he had the courage to believe them.'

That was true. She forced herself to straighten and shake off the sadness settling over her.

'Can I read it?'

She blinked when Nikos gestured to the diary, but she passed it to him without a word. He'd treat her great-aunt's words with respect. Besides, as both she and Siena had read it, it only seemed fair that Nikos and Christian should have the opportunity too.

Pulling in a breath, she tried to smile. 'Your grandfather must've been happy, though, when you told him you might be able to win back the Ananke necklace.'

A tic started at the base of his jaw. 'I didn't tell him.'

What? If he hadn't told his grandfather about the necklace... Her heart thudded so hard she could barely think over the pounding. Did that mean that maybe she did have a chance? That maybe Nikos would choose her over the necklace?

Or was that just wishful thinking?

'I didn't exactly get the chance to tell him. He demanded an explanation for why you and I were travelling together, and when he found out that Christian and Siena might already be engaged...' He grimaced.

It was clear the two men had exchanged words, but Nikos could've calmed his grandfather down with that single revelation—that he was in the process of winning back the Ananke necklace. Yet he'd chosen not to.

She shouldn't read too much into it, but her foolish heart leapt with hope anyway. She fought to keep the expression on her face even. 'Did you want to head back to the mainland this afternoon?'

'We wouldn't make it before nightfall. We'll leave in the morning as planned.'

MJ was already at the jetty the following morning when Nikos strode down from the house. She took in his long-legged, lean-hipped stride and had to look away, her hunger for him taking her off-guard. They'd eaten together last night, but his grandfather hadn't shown his face again. They'd spent an oddly restful evening in the living room, Nikos working and MJ reading.

This morning, a maid had brought a breakfast tray to her room with a note from Nikos saying he wanted to leave within the hour.

'My grandfather did some digging,' he said without preamble. 'Christian and Siena are in London.'

'London?'

'Apparently they never left.'

He handed her a scrap of paper. Scrawled across it was the name of a London medical clinic. MJ fought a sudden desire to laugh. Siena had been seeking treatment at home all this time. She pressed the slip of paper to her chest. 'How soon…?'

'We should be in Athens by ten, and we've a one o'clock flight from there to London.'

'Perfect!' It took everything she had not to throw her arms around his neck. 'And, Nikos?'

He swung back from where he'd jumped on deck, his hair ruffling in the gentle breeze. 'Yes?'

'Thank you.'

He held out his hand to help her on board. 'Any time, MJ. Any time.'

And she knew he meant it.

MJ pulled to a halt outside Siena's room and ran a hand down the front of her shirt.

'What's wrong?' Nikos asked, instantly alert.

He'd been watching her carefully since they'd left Athens, and his concern warmed her all the way through.

'Don't you want to go in?'

'I need to go in. I have to assure myself she's okay. It's just…' She bit back a sigh. 'I'm starting to wonder if I should've left it all well enough alone and trusted her.' She had no idea how her sister was going to react to seeing her so unexpectedly, and the thought made her stomach churn. Standing out there delaying the moment wouldn't help matters, though.

'I have your back, MJ. You know that, don't you?'

She did. And it helped. Pulling in a breath, she sent him a smile and forced back her shoulders. 'Here goes.'

Not giving herself a chance to think any further, she knocked on the door and then strode into the room. Siena reclined in a hospital bed, pillows piled up at her back. There was colour in her cheeks and a sparkle in her eyes. She wasn't hooked up to a multitude of machines or with a variety of tubes protruding from her arms as MJ had feared. The relief nearly knocked her off her feet.

Siena's face lit up. 'Jojo!'

MJ raced over and hugged her. Gently at first, but then with the same fierceness that Siena did her. Eventually she eased back and held her sister at arm's length, scanning her from head to toe. 'You're okay?'

'As good as new, I promise. One of Christian's best friends is a doctor here and he agreed to see me as a favour. They did some super-minor surgery and my results are great. I'll be released in a day or two. I probably could've gone home a couple of days ago, but…'

She broke off, reddening.

'But you were hiding out.'

'We just wanted a little peace…some calm before all hell broke loose.' Siena squeezed her hand, her eyes pleading. 'You can understand that, can't you?' She held up her left hand. An engagement ring sparkled on her finger. 'And hell *is* going to break loose.'

'I'm very happy for you both. Congratulations.' She fought the lump in her throat to squeeze Siena's hand and smile at Christian, who'd been sitting in the chair beside Siena's bed, but had risen at her entrance.

Siena's smile faltered. 'Jojo?'

'I'm happy for you, Sisi, but couldn't you have sent me just one text to tell me you were well and getting the treatment you needed? You had to know how worried I'd be.'

'I was afraid if I did that you'd search all the hospitals in London. And I wasn't ready to share our news with anyone.'

'How could you have been so inconsiderate?' Nikos burst out from behind her. 'MJ nearly made herself sick worrying about you. She thought you were in serious danger!'

Siena's eyes widened. 'From Christian?'

'From your health!' he roared. 'She thought you might be dying!'

Oh, whoa. *Wow.* Before MJ could try and calm him, Christian bristled. 'You can shut it right now, Nik. You don't get to speak to my fiancée that way, you hear me? Siena's had surgery and she needs to rest. The last thing she needs is anyone upsetting her.'

With a muffled oath, Nikos swung away and stalked across to the other side of the room to stare out of the window.

'I'm sorry, Jojo,' Siena whispered. 'I thought when Freddy told you I was in a clinic in Switzerland that it would set your mind at rest.'

To be fair, it had eased it. But it hadn't dispelled her fears completely.

'And I'm so glad you're here now.' Siena

gripped her hand. 'We need your help. Neither of our families is going to approve of the match—everyone is going to be against us marrying—and no one smoothes ruffled feathers like you. And—'

'No.' MJ stood from where she'd been sitting on the side of the bed and tugged her hand from Siena's. 'If you love Christian, you fight for him. You'll always have my support. You're my sister and I love you. But this is your fight—yours and Christian's.'

Siena's mouth dropped open. 'Is this because you're angry with me?'

The accusation made MJ blink, but then she nodded. 'I guess I am angry with you. You hurt me more than you know.'

Siena's gaze dropped. 'I'm sorry. I—'

'But I'll get over it, and that isn't what this is about anyway. You said I always come to your rescue, and it's true. I do. I'm sorry, but you don't get to pick and choose when to stand on your own two feet and then abdicate responsibility back to me when it all feels too hard. That's not how being a fully functioning adult works.'

'But…'

When Siena didn't continue, MJ soldiered on. 'I'm also sorry if I made you feel like some kind of sticking plaster because I was missing Mother.' Her heart pounded all the way up into her throat. 'I didn't mean to make you feel like that.'

Siena gave a sob and Christian put an arm around her shoulders. It was odd to see someone else comfort her sister, but they looked right together.

She made herself smile. 'What happened between Aunt Joan and Vasillios Constantinos happened fifty years ago. You'll just have to show everyone that's all in the past. My advice, for what it's worth, is act with integrity, treat everyone with as much consideration and generosity as you can and try to keep your tempers when other people lose theirs. If you can manage to not fly off the handle and act in a reasonable and rational manner, then—'

'That's the problem, though, Jojo!' Siena burst out. 'It's not really in the past at all!'

What was she talking about?

'Oh, Jojo, *our parents*!'

She went cold all over, recalling Nikos's warning that she didn't know the entire story. She turned to glance at him now, but he didn't turn towards her, didn't meet her gaze, and that made her go even colder. 'What about our parents?' she demanded, swinging back.

'Father had an affair with Tori Constantinos.'

MJ's breath jammed. She took a step back. *No!* Surely not? It...

The room spun. The ongoing hatred... Dear God, it made perfect sense. Why had their father kept this from them? Her temples pounded and her eyes burned. Why hadn't *Nikos* told her?

'When Andreas found out...'

Siena broke off to grip Christian's hand with both of her own.

Andreas? Nikos's father? 'Go on.' MJ's voice didn't sound as if it belonged to her.

'He phoned mother...' Siena's voice wobbled. 'And told her. Told her where their assignations took place, told her that's where her cheating husband was right at that current moment in time. That's where mother was driving to, Jojo, when she had the car accident that killed her. She had the accident because she was so upset.'

What?

'Father and Andreas...they hate each other even more than Aunt Joan and Vasillios did. Do you now see what we're up against?'

MJ had to brace a hand against the wall to stop from falling. Siena threw off her covers as if to come to her, but MJ shook her head. 'None of you touch me.'

A sob caught in Siena's throat that found an echo in her own chest. Christian gestured her to the chair he'd been sitting in, but instead she moved to a chair on the other side of the room, one away from everyone else.

All this time, Nikos had known, and yet he hadn't...

Her chest splintered as if a spear had been

thrown through it. She tried to focus on Siena's words rather than the sense of betrayal that threatened her composure. All of this time, Nikos had known and yet he'd kept it from her.

Don't. Not yet.

She forced up her chin. 'I'm sorry, Siena, but you're wrong.'

Tears spilled down Siena's cheeks, but she shook her head. 'It's the truth, Jojo. I know it's shocking, but—'

'It wasn't a man's voice on the phone that day.'

From the corner of her eye, she saw Nikos freeze. She did what she could to block him out.

'It wasn't Andreas who told Mother about the affair. It was Tori.'

Christian's face twisted and his hands clenched. 'That's a lie!'

'You were at art class,' MJ continued as if Christian hadn't spoken. 'And I was having a cooking lesson with Mother. Alice was busy signing for a delivery, and Mother's hands were sticky with cookie dough, so when the phone rang I answered it while Mother washed her hands.

'When she came to the phone, she listened for bit and then yelled at the person at the other end, said they were lying, before slamming the receiver back down. And then she grabbed her car keys and told Alice to finish helping me make the cookies and left.' She pushed her hair from her face with a shaky hand. Clenching it, she dragged it back into her lap. 'It was the last time I saw her alive.'

'You're lying!' Christian's eyes had gone wild. He stared from MJ to his brother. 'Father told me he was the one who called Diana…and how he regretted it, how he wished he'd kept the information to himself.'

'She's not lying, Christian.'

Nikos's words made her want to lie on the floor and sleep for a very long time. Apparently he knew the *whole* truth.

'Father's the one who lied,' he went on.

'Why?'

'To protect Mother. He loved her. She'd rung Diana in an attempt to break up the Mabels' marriage so she and Graham could be together. There was no chance of that happening, though, once Diana had the car accident. In taking the blame for it, Father hoped she'd stay with him rather than give up on their marriage.'

Christian fell down into his chair. Siena pressed a hand to her mouth.

MJ stood and started for the door, emotion boiling, thrashing and whipping at her.

'Where are you going?'

The panic in Siena's voice barely touched her. Still, she turned to meet her sister's gaze. 'I'm going home.'

'But you can't. We—'

'I can!'

The force of her words had Siena's and Christian's jaws dropping. Not Nikos's, though. But every single muscle he had tensed and she hated that she was so attuned to him. So attuned when he'd *lied to her*!

She thumped a hand to her chest. 'I gave you all the best of me—the *very* best. But that doesn't seem to have had any impact on you at all.' She met Nikos's eyes. 'It doesn't seem to have *mattered* to you at all.'

He'd gone grey beneath his tan. She hoped he felt one-tenth as sick as she did.

'I'm taking a time-out. I want some...*space*.'

While she didn't exactly spit out that last word, it emerged with an edge she couldn't temper.

'Oh, Jojo.' Siena hiccupped. 'Please...'

All this time Nikos had known!

'I'm tired of everyone's petty grievances—the way you all deliberately nurse and feed your sense of injury, and all of the wailing, bitching and moaning. I've had enough of it. *All of it!* You can sort it out on your own, because I'm out. I'm not having a bar of it any more.'

And with that she strode out of the door before she started crying.

Nikos made the mistake of following her. She could feel him even before he spoke. 'Let me take you home.'

Not on her life...

Seizing his arm, she hauled him into a thankfully empty waiting room.

'You knew.' She dropped his arm. She could only whisper because a lump had lodged in her throat. Speaking hurt her, but words bubbled up anyway. 'All this time you knew about the affair between my mother and your father and you never told me.'

He dragged a hand down his face. 'God help me, MJ. I'm sorry. So sorry. At first I couldn't believe you didn't know and then…'

She spread her hands, forcing her eyes wide in mockery. 'And then what? You didn't think I had a right to know? Didn't think I'd want to know?'

'Hell, MJ!' He paced the length of the room and then swung back. 'At first it didn't seem my place to tell you. It seemed a cruel thing to do.'

Anger dissolved the lump in her throat. *Cruel?* Heat scalded the backs of her eyes and burned a hole through the middle of her heart. She refused to let a single tear fall. Not here. Not now. Not in front of *him*. 'You slept with me, but all the time you kept this huge secret from me? I can't even…'

She folded her arms to hide the way her hands shook. 'Was this about revenge after all? Was me promising you the Ananke necklace not enough?'

Crimson stained his cheekbones. 'No! I never wanted revenge on you. I *never* wanted to hurt you. I wish to God I'd done things differently. I wish I could turn the clocks back.'

But he couldn't. And why should she believe him anyway? She'd laid herself bare to this man, but he hadn't done the same. She was a fool. A bigger fool than even her Aunt Joan.

'I care about you, Marjorie.'

Very slowly, she shook her head. 'I don't believe you. Someone who cared for me would never have lied to me the way you did.' She forced her chin up. 'What an idiot I've been. I should've recognised it from the first. Everyone else did.'

'Recognised what?'

The words croaked from him. His face was haggard, his spine and shoulders sagging as if they'd lost the ability to hold themselves up. He looked as sick and wretched as she felt. Maybe he was sorry. But it didn't change the cold, hard facts. What had happened aboard the yacht had obviously meant a lot more to her than it ever had to him.

She enunciated the words clearly. 'I didn't recognise that you're exactly like your grandfather... and your father...and my father.'

His head rocked back, his eyes going wild. He opened his mouth.

'And now maybe I am too. Thanks to you.'

He bent at the waist then, bracing his hands on his knees as if she'd dealt him a body blow.

'I'll see myself home, thank you, Nikos.'

She swept past him and didn't look back.

CHAPTER ELEVEN

'Ms Marjorie Mabel to see you, sir.'

Nikos shot out of his chair. *MJ? Here?*

She'd not answered a single one of his calls, texts or emails yesterday. He knew he needed to give her time, but the guilt had torn at him. And knowing how much she was hurting had slashed him inside out.

He deserved to be dying a thousand deaths, not *her*.

He had to find a way to make things right. He had to find a way to make her see that he'd never meant to hurt her. 'Don't keep her waiting, Giles. I—'

'He hasn't kept me waiting, Nikos.'

MJ emerged from behind his assistant and Nikos's heart thundered in his ears. He rounded the desk to take her hands. Giles left, closing the door behind him.

Damn it! She looked pale and wan. Dark circles stretched beneath her eyes like bruises. 'How are you?'

She raised an eyebrow and he winced. 'Sorry, that was a stupid question.' He led her to a chair and took the one opposite, not relinquishing her hand. 'I can't tell you how good it is to see you,

MJ. And I know I don't deserve it, but will you give me a chance to try and explain?'

She bit her lip and glanced away, pulling her hand from his and folding in on herself. He recognised the misery and found himself on his knees in front of her. 'Marjorie, please. I swear I never meant to hurt you. I'd rather cut off my own arm.'

Her eyes widened at whatever she saw in his face.

'What you've been trying to do—wanting to bring an end to the feud.' He pressed a hand to his chest. 'I admire it with all my heart. I want to make that happen too.' Nausea churned in his gut. 'If you now hate me with the same savagery as the past generations have hated each other…'

Bitterness filled his mouth and coated his tongue. He didn't know how he'd bear it. To know he'd taken something so beautiful and destroyed it…

'I don't hate you, Nikos.'

She gestured to the seat opposite, and he forced himself to take it.

'Why did you keep the truth from me? Why did you lie?'

He scrubbed both hands through his hair. How the hell did he explain it to her?

Start at the beginning…

'I didn't know about my mother and Graham's affair until after your mother's car accident. My father bundled the entire family off to the Devon house.'

'Away from prying eyes,' she murmured in a monotone.

'Their fights—' He broke off, breathing hard, not entirely sure how to describe them. 'I'd never heard anything like them before, had never witnessed anything so *raw*. I didn't know what to do, didn't know how to help.'

All he'd wanted to do was put his family back together. He'd come to hate Graham Mabel with every atom of his being that summer. He'd blamed the man for everything. It'd made sense when he'd been fourteen, but now...

He let out a long breath. 'I didn't know grown men—tough men like my father and grandfather—could cry. But my father cried...and he begged my mother to stay. He begged her not to abandon her family. He told her he'd take the blame, that he'd tell Graham he'd been the one to ring Diana, if only she'd stay.'

Two deep furrows carved themselves into MJ's brow. 'And she let him?'

His head felt too heavy for his shoulders. 'I think a part of her still hoped that, if your father never knew she'd been the one to reveal the truth of the affair to Diana, there'd still be a chance for them, but...' He dragged a hand down his face. 'She was in shock, traumatised. She was never the same again. She sure as hell wasn't thinking clearly.'

MJ rubbed a hand across her chest.

'She agreed to stay. And she tried, she really did, but the guilt ate at her.' He was quiet for a moment, his heart thumping. 'She tried to take her own life. It was only my grandfather's quick thinking and knowledge of CPR that saved her life.'

Understanding dawned in her eyes. 'That's why you feel you owe your grandfather such a debt.'

He shook his head. Not in denial, but it wasn't the full truth either. 'I've always loved my grandfather. He's been good to me.' But there was no denying that, because he'd saved Nikos's mother's life, they'd all felt a deeper debt to the older man.

'After her suicide attempt, I confronted my father and told him I knew the truth. I wanted him to tell Christian the truth too—that it'd been Mother not him who'd told Diana about the affair—but he refused. He swore me to secrecy; made me swear not to tell a living soul—not my grandfather and not my brother.'

Her frown deepened and she leaned towards him. 'You were only fourteen. It's not fair to ask a fourteen-year-old to bear that kind of burden.'

It hadn't felt particularly onerous until he'd met MJ. He'd wanted to protect his fragile mother from gossip and scandal, and he'd wanted to help his father save face. But once he'd met MJ... 'I'm sorry I didn't tell you. I should've at least told you about the affair, even if I couldn't tell you the whole truth. But…'

She glanced up.

'I was afraid that, once I started, I'd reveal everything.'

'Who to betray—me or your father?' She pulled in a breath and let it out again in a slow whoosh. 'I'm glad I wasn't in your shoes, Nikos.'

'I know how betrayed you felt yesterday, MJ.'

Her gaze dropped.

'And in that moment I hated myself. If I could do things over, I'd tell you everything.'

'My own father should've told me.' She stared at her hands and grimaced. 'I feel I was unnecessarily harsh to you at the hospital and I'm sorry.'

'Don't you dare apologise.' His voice shook from the force of his emotion. 'You're the one person in this whole sorry mess who doesn't need to apologise to anyone.'

He hesitated. He deserved her animosity and revulsion, but… 'You don't hate me.'

She glanced up.

'And you don't hate my father.'

'I don't hate anyone.' One slim shoulder lifted. 'How can I hate Tori, Andreas and Father when they've all paid for what happened back then a thousand times over? What happened was dreadful, but none of them would've meant for my mother to die. I can hardly imagine the guilt and regret they've all carried since then. No wonder our fathers never remarried, Nikos.'

The depth of her empathy, and her ability and *willingness* to forgive, astounded him. Shamed him. For years he'd mindlessly hated her father and great-aunt because of the pain they'd inflicted on his family. But his family had inflicted just as much pain on hers in its turn.

'And I can see how badly you feel too, Nikos. But you should never have been put in this a situation in the first place.'

'How do you do it?' he burst out. 'How can you be so forgiving and tolerant of other people's weaknesses? How do you do that and still manage to care about everyone so much?'

'You make me sound like a saint.' She sprang to her feet. 'I'm not! I feel angry with everyone sometimes.' She flung out an arm and paced about the room. 'I have to fight the urge to not shake everyone, and their preoccupation with dwelling on drama and the ill feeling and being double-crossed and feeling ill-used.… I want to yell at everyone to just *get over it*!'

She slammed herself back into her chair. 'The truth is I spent a lot of time with Aunt Joan. What she and Vasillios allowed to happen between them horrified me. If only they'd had the courage to swallow their pride they'd have won *everything*. I swore to never make the same mistake.'

Most people refused to take risks because they

were afraid of the consequences. MJ was the opposite. She took risks because she refused to live a life of regret.

'I'm demanding everyone be the best damn person they can be, and I'm not sure that's fair, let alone possible.' She blew out a breath and met his gaze. 'But I still can't help feeling it's necessary.'

An ache stretched through him. He didn't know if it was possible either. But they could make a start on improving things, couldn't they? That was better than nothing.

Her face lost some of its light, as if she'd read his scepticism. 'I have something for you.' Reaching into her handbag, she pulled out a parcel and held it towards him.

He took it in numb fingers, pulled off the plain paper packaging and lifted the lid of a wooden box. His breath bunched beneath his breastbone, every muscle clenching when he saw what was nestled there. *The Ananke necklace.*

'The lawyer wouldn't let me take it until I'd signed a declaration to say I was bringing it directly to you. I wanted to give it to you personally. I wanted to thank you for all you did, for all of your help and kindness. You kept your word and fulfilled our bargain to the letter. I'm very grateful.'

She was going to leave, and if he didn't find the right thing to say he might never see her again! He shot to his feet. 'This can't be goodbye, MJ.'

She rose. 'We'll see each other around, of course, and—'

'I want to keep seeing you. I want to date you.' He wanted to kiss her again.

She set her handbag and jacket on the seat of her chair before glancing at the necklace he held. 'You're planning to use that to buy your family's acceptance of Christian and Siena's engagement, aren't you?'

He nodded. He couldn't see any other way round it. 'But it can buy acceptance for us too, MJ. We can work this out.'

She strode to the window and stared out of it for several long moments before turning, her hands pressed to her stomach. 'Let me give you a hypothetical situation, Nikos. Let's just say, for argument's sake, that I love you. Which, for the record, is true.'

Her words electrified him. Before he could say anything, she continued.

'And let's say you love me too.' She held up both hands. 'Please don't answer that, as either answer will break my heart.' She dragged in a breath that made her whole body tremble. 'And let's say we married and had three adorable children...'

'You want three children?'

The smallest of smiles touched her lips. 'Three sounds like a nice number.'

That smile faded. 'Less nice, however, is if one of the children adored their maternal grandfather, heard our family's history from his perspective and sympathised, while another one heard it from his paternal grandfather and sympathised with that perspective instead. The two of them then start fighting over which of them should inherit the necklace.'

She raised her chin and met his gaze. 'Who do we give it to, Nikos? That kind of thing splits families up. *That's* why I won't have the necklace in my life, even if it means walking away from you.'

She gathered up her things, paused and then very quietly slipped a smooth pink pebble onto his desk. 'Goodbye, Nikos.'

He stared at the pebble and had a swift memory of her bending down on their Greek island to pick it up.

He opened his mouth, but what could he say?

She walked through the door without halting. Walked away from him. And it was as if every good thing he'd ever known had been taken from him.

He flung the priceless necklace across the room and lowered himself onto his chair, closing a fist around the pebble.

MJ walked through the door of her Chelsea flat and halted. Turning on the spot, she searched for…*something*…but she had no idea what.

Whatever. She had a feeling it couldn't be found here anyway.

She had a feeling it couldn't be found any-where.

'Marjorie Joan Mabel, what have you done?'

Tossing her handbag on the hall table, she tried to rub warmth into her arms, her hands moving briskly up and down, but she barely felt them. She'd gone numb all over.

'And, if you're going to start talking to your-self, it might be an idea to get a cat so the neigh-bours don't think you're an absolute loser.'

A warm and cuddly cat in the flat might be comforting. But the thought of cats had her think-ing of dogs, specifically Seth and Rufus, Nikos's dogs in Devon. Which, of course, had her think-ing, yet again, about Nikos.

She dropped down to the sofa and hugged a cushion to her chest. Had she really just walked away from him? She held the cushion at arm's length.

'Am I demanding too much? Am I being just like Vasillios and Aunt Joan and Tori Constan-tinos?'

She threw the cushion to one side and dropped her head in her hands. Was she letting her ha-tred of the feud and all of the fighting between their two families skew her judgement? Nikos was right. Between them, they *could* improve things. Wasn't that a worthy goal, something to be celebrated? Why couldn't that be enough? Why couldn't she be content with that?

But she couldn't be satisfied. It wasn't enough.

The cold, uncompromising relentlessness of that thought dropped down on her, a guillotine blade severing any hope of finding a way to make a relationship work with the man she loved.

For as long as one or the other of their families had possession of the Ananke necklace, the possibility of new hostilities breaking out remained. She'd made a promise to herself and to Aunt Joan to have nothing to do with either.

In her heart of hearts, she knew she was making the right decision. That didn't stop her heart from feeling like a dead, black weight in her chest, though. She hadn't known the price she'd have to pay would be so high.

Curling up on her side, she drew her knees to her chest and stared unseeingly at the room as the shadows lengthened, her eyes burning and her throat aching.

'What did you want to see me about, MJ?'

Her father had *that* look on his face—the 'I don't want any more lectures about your sister' look.

It had been less than a fortnight since she'd last seen him, and in that time it appeared nothing had changed for him. While for her it felt as if her whole life had been turned upside down.

Well, this should be fun.

She closed the office door behind her and

squared her shoulders. 'This would've been better said in the privacy of the family home, but as you insisted you had no time to see me out of hours, and to make an appointment with your PA to see you during business hours instead, I'm not going to apologise for it.'

'If this is about Siena—'

'I've given the Ananke necklace to Nikos Constantinos.'

He stared as if he didn't understand the words she'd just uttered. And she didn't give him time to gather his scattered wits.

'I also know what happened between you and Tori Constantinos eighteen years ago—that the two of you were having an affair.'

She sat without being invited and watched the colour leach from his face. A part of her ached for him, but mostly she just felt numb.

'MJ, I...' He swallowed.

'You destroyed the Constantinos marriage.' Not single-handedly—Tori had had a hand in that too—but it was a fact, plain and simple.

'And now you hold me responsible for your mother's death.'

The words dropped from him. She saw his guilt then and her heart burned. She reached across the table as if to touch him, but the expanse of desk was too wide. 'No.' She shook her head. 'No.'

His chin came up and his eyes flashed. 'Then why else would you punish me and give the

Ananke necklace to a member of *that family*?' He spat the words, investing 'that family' with as much loathing as he could. 'There are things you don't know, MJ, things that would change the way you—'

'I know you hold Andreas responsible for Mother's death. You think he rang her and told her about the affair, told her where you and Tori met. Told her that's where the two of you were that afternoon, the same afternoon she had her accident. I know that you think, if she hadn't been so distraught, she'd not have had the accident.'

'It's true! Andreas…'

She shook her head.

He leapt up. 'It is! And—'

'I answered the phone that day.'

He stared at her as if her words made no sense.

'I know I was only nine, but I remember. I remember everything about that afternoon.' It was the last afternoon she'd spent with her mother. It was burned on her brain. 'It wasn't Andreas who called, Father. It was Tori.'

His mouth worked but no sound came out. He lowered himself back to his chair as if any sudden movement would shatter him. 'But, when I accused him, Andreas didn't deny it.'

'What would you have done in his shoes? You'd destroyed his marriage—he wanted to strike back. And he wanted to protect Tori.'

'But why would Tori…?' He swallowed and

very slowly nodded. 'She wanted to leave Andreas. She wanted me to leave your mother.'

'Were you in love with her?' Had he loved her as fiercely as she did Nikos?

'I…yes.' He dragged a hand down his face, looking haggard and old. 'Your mother was my best friend, MJ, but we'd married young and…' He spread his hands, helplessly mute. 'With Tori, I had never known passion like it. The adultery was unforgivable. I should have confessed all to your mother immediately. But I didn't. And when she died…' His mouth firmed. 'I didn't deserve happiness after that.'

'What a mess you all made of it.'

For once her father didn't argue, but he thrust out his jaw. 'Nikos told you all this? Made you feel guilty so you would give him the necklace?'

'Nikos is a decent man. He actually tried to protect me from the truth. It was Siena and Christian who told me.'

His mouth worked. 'What the hell is Siena doing with Christian Constantinos?'

'Siena's last test results weren't good.'

He straightened, his gaze sharpening. 'Dear God.'

'She went to ground and I couldn't find her. I offered Nikos the necklace in exchange for helping me find her.'

'Why did you not tell me of this?'

'I told you repeatedly to ring her!' She shouted

the words, surprising them both. 'What if that fight was the last conversation you ever had with her? How would you have felt? *Have you learned nothing from the past?*'

He shot to his feet. 'Is she—?'

'She's fine.' She worked hard to get her frustration back under control, forcing herself back into her seat. 'Christian took her to a private clinic. She's responded well to treatment. By the way, she and Christian are engaged. So here's your chance to finally act well and make amends.'

Disbelief overturned his relief. 'A union between the Mabels and the Constantinoses can never happen. It won't work. I forbid it. It'll end in disaster and—'

'It's going to happen whether you like it or not.' She rose. 'If you don't want to tear our family apart, I suggest you find a way to make it work.' As she spoke, she strode to the door. She turned when she reached it. 'Or we lose.' Her gaze collided with his. 'You need to decide what matters more to you—this feud or your children.'

And then she left. She'd already lost, but it didn't mean Siena and Christian couldn't find happiness.

If worst came to worst, Siena and their father would never speak to each other again... The vision of being torn at Christmases and birthdays rose in her mind. Her stomach churned. It was the likeliest outcome. As much as she hated to admit it, it was probably what the future held.

Unless everyone found the strength to act as their best selves.

Ha! As if that had ever happened between the Mabel and Constantinos families.

MJ had done her best to set out the facts as starkly as she could, to make sure everyone knew what was at stake. She had no other bright ideas now for how to heal the rift. She'd failed.

When she finally got home she let herself into her flat, kicking off her shoes and letting her handbag slide off her shoulder to land on the floor beside them. Falling down to the sofa, she grabbed the cushion and held it at arm's length. She *really* needed to get a cat.

'Do you think, if I asked him, Nikos would emigrate to New Zealand with me? Somewhere far, far away from all of this trouble and strife...'

She shook her head. 'Me neither.' A lump lodged in her throat. Clutching the cushion to her chest, she concentrated on breathing through the waves of pain that tried to swallow her.

CHAPTER TWELVE

NIKOS SPENT THE best part of the following week trying to erase the time he'd spent with MJ from his mind. While he might never have met a woman who'd affected him as much, their time together had been ephemeral, fleeting—a brief moment of perfection, neither permanent nor durable. It wasn't something they could build on. She'd made that very clear.

He buried himself in work, and in the evenings he read Joan's diary. It made him feel closer to MJ, but it didn't lift the heavy weight that pressed his heart flat, sapping his energy and draining all enjoyment from his days.

On the sixth day he gave up the pretence. He strode around his office and swore—his office in the city, rather than his office at home, because whenever he worked from home now he found himself continually waiting for MJ to burst in, and being disappointed when she didn't.

Damn it all to hell! MJ had told him she loved him. He could try and hide from the truth, but what good would it do? He loved her back, body and soul. Every second was an agony of missing her, aching for her and craving her.

He swore again. Louder this time. He knew

how much she'd be hurting. She didn't deserve that pain. In this whole sorry mess, she was the only person who'd acted with integrity. She didn't deserve a broken heart. She deserved a medal!

Then give her what she wants.

He rested his forehead against the cool glass of a window, not noticing the busy cityscape below or the distant view of the iconic dome of St Paul's Cathedral. What MJ wanted was impossible. How could he give her what she wanted while remaining true to his family, and without tearing his family apart?

His mother's betrayal with Graham Mabel had shattered his father. For God's sake, his grandfather had saved Tori when she'd tried to take her own life. Both men deserved peace, not more upheaval and trauma.

As long as either one of our families owns the necklace, there will be no peace.

He could hear MJ's voice in his head as clearly as if she stood in the office with him. The scenario she'd presented him with—of their feuding children—had truly horrified him.

Of course, it was a hypothetical situation. Who knew if such an eventuality would ever come to pass? But, for as long as their families continued to squabble over the necklace's ownership, the possibility remained. His hands fisted. Was this the legacy they'd now pass onto any children Christian and Siena might have?

Acid burned his gut. MJ had been right to want to banish the necklace from her life, from all their lives, but he couldn't see a way to make that happen.

Unless…

He froze. Unless he could bridge the many gulfs that lay between the Constantinoses and the Mabels.

His heart pounded. The odds weren't in his favour. There wasn't any point in fooling himself about that. But what was the alternative—let MJ go?

No!

If there was the slightest chance of winning MJ's heart, and giving her the future she so desperately wanted, then anything was worth a shot. He clenched and unclenched his hands. He might not succeed, but…

If he didn't at least try, then he didn't deserve her.

And he wanted to deserve her. More than he'd ever wanted anything in his life.

Seizing the phone from his desk, he rang his grandfather.

'Have you talked sense into that fool brother of yours yet?' the older man demanded. 'I won't—'

'I've rung to tell you that I have the Ananke necklace.'

Silence greeted his pronouncement, but he heard his grandfather's quick intake of breath.

'MJ gave it to me. It's mine, fair and square. I even have a signed contract to prove it.'

'You…but… I never thought I'd live to see this day! Nikos, you make an old man very happy and—'

'But unless you agree to read Joan Mabel's diary I'm going to give it back.'

'How dare you? I'm your grandfather. You cannot give me ultimatums—'

'I'm not even going to discuss this with you, Pappoús. I'm emailing the scanned diary pages to you right now. I'll ring back in five days and hope to find you've read them.'

He ended the call and then tapped his fingers against the warm walnut of his desk. Pressing the intercom, he ordered his PA to make an appointment for him to meet with Graham Mabel.

She hesitated. 'Graham Mabel, sir?'

'That's right. For as soon as it can be arranged. And an appointment with the lawyer Bayard Crawford. And cancel all of my appointments for this afternoon.'

'Yes, sir.'

His mind raced to the next task—Siena and Christian. Grabbing his coat from the back of his chair, he strode from the office. He'd go and see them in person.

Ten days later Nikos strode into MJ's office, not giving her PA the opportunity to announce him.

MJ glanced up from her computer and her jaw dropped. *'Nikos!'*

Everything inside him protested at her pallor, at the dark circles under her eyes. Had she lost weight? She needed to look after herself!

He planted himself into the chair opposite. 'Can you call your PA off, please, MJ? Tell her she doesn't need to call security to have me thrown out?'

'It's okay, Lucy.' She nodded to her PA. 'Mr Constantinos and I are…'

His heart beat hard.

A smile touched her lips and it lightened everything inside him. 'Old friends.'

God, he loved this woman! She might look tired, she might look worn thin, but her smile told him she was glad to see him. It didn't hold even the faintest edge of resentment or bitterness.

She turned back to him, lifted her hands and let them drop. 'This is a surprise.'

His heart burned. While there might not be any resentment in her smile, it wasn't pain-free. She hid it well, but he'd come to know her heart almost as well as he knew his own. He yearned to replace that pain with joy.

'What can I do for you?'

She was trying to be business-like and professional, but the way her gaze momentarily dropped from his, the way her chest lifted as she pulled in a steadying breath, told him she was having as hard a time as him at reining in her emotions.

'I've missed you,' he found himself murmuring. 'I wanted to see you.'

She swallowed. 'Nikos—'

'I *needed* to see you.'

Her eyes flashed then. She laid her hands flat on the desk. 'I didn't think you were cruel or selfish. This can't happen, Nikos. I've explained why. I understand that you might not agree with me, but I've told you how I feel and you have to respect that, accept that.'

'I will always do my best to accept and respect the way you feel, MJ, but I don't have to necessarily accept how other people feel or act if I think they're wrong.'

Her brow pleated. 'You think I'm wrong?'

No, he thought her magnificent. 'I think your reading of our situation is spot on.'

A tiny light in her eyes died. She moistened her lips and nodded.

He reached into his pocket, pulled out the box containing the Ananke necklace and set it on her desk.

Her nose wrinkled. 'What on earth are you doing bringing *that* into my office?'

He almost laughed out loud. Any other woman would've fawned over the necklace but not MJ. 'I think your reading of our situation is spot on, but I don't think anyone else's is.'

Her gaze flew back to his. 'What does that mean?'

'It *means*,' he said with deliberate emphasis, 'that I've bullied, cajoled, blackmailed and harangued every member of our respective families until they've seen sense.'

Her eyes went wide. She shot to her feet, her hands gripping each other in a white-knuckled clench. 'Including my father and Siena?'

'Yes.'

'How…? But…? Why haven't I heard about any of this from either one of them then?'

He stood too. 'From all accounts, you've been keeping a low profile these last couple of weeks, haven't been seeing anyone.'

She opened her mouth, closed it and shrugged. 'I haven't been feeling all that sociable.'

'MJ, I—'

'So that means…' She pressed the heels of her hands to her temples, frowning. 'Oh, Nikos, I never wanted you to estrange yourself from your family! I know how much you love them, how protective you are of them, and how you want to save them from further pain and suffering. I understand that and—'

'The only way I can truly protect them, and any future generations, is to bring this godforsaken feud to an end once and for all. And to do that we need to get rid of this.' He pointed to the necklace.

Striding round the desk, he took her hand.

'Come.' He led her to the sofa on the other side of the room. 'I have much to tell you and I also need your signature.'

'My signature?' She sat but glanced back at her desk. 'I don't want that damn necklace, Nikos, so don't even think about giving it back to me.'

This time he did laugh out loud.

'I mean it. I—' She broke off and bit her lip. 'Though, if you do give it back, I guess I can finally donate it and we can all be rid of it.'

'I told my grandfather that unless he read Joan's journal I'd do exactly that and give it back.'

'I—' She shook herself. 'What did he do?'

'He read the journal.'

She rubbed a hand across her chest. 'Was he okay afterwards?' She leaned towards him. 'Please tell me it helped him to find peace.'

It took all of his strength not to take her face in his hands and kiss her.

She touched his arm. 'It hasn't hurt your relationship with him, has it?'

He pressed his hand over hers, grasping that small warmth to himself. 'No, we're good. You don't need to worry about that. But it did send him on a hell of a journey—made him question all he thought he knew. Regret, shame, anger have all been part of that journey. But your great-aunt's final words to him...' He paused, recalling the expression in his grandfather's eyes when he'd spoken to Nikos about it. 'They didn't just bring him peace, MJ, they brought him joy.'

Her lips curved in a smile that could have made a man's heart beat a path out of his chest. 'I'm so glad.'

He'd never seen his grandfather joyful before. Pleased and satisfied, yes. Proud, determined and angry, yes. But never joyful. It had been a gift.

'The thing is, MJ, I started to realise there was a flaw in this plan of yours to donate the necklace. The fact is, the power would always remain with the party who did the donating.'

She glanced at her hand on his forearm, his hand resting on top of it. She squeezed gently and then pulled her hand back to her lap. 'I don't mind if you donate it. I can reconcile my family to that.'

She'd try to, but a shadow would always remain.

Some of the light went out of her eyes when he remained silent. 'You want to keep it.' The words were flat, dull...lifeless.

'You misunderstand me.'

She raised an eyebrow.

'I don't want to keep the necklace, but if I went ahead and donated it that'd merely remove the object of all the resentment, not the resentment itself. If we truly want to fix things, we have to address the heart of the problems. If donating the necklace is the wisest course of action for our families, and I think it is, we need everyone to agree to it.'

Her eyes widened.

'We need to reconcile my grandfather to your great-aunt, and our fathers to one another. The journal worked its magic on my grandfather. He signed the contract I have here.' He pulled the folded contract from his top pocket and set it on the coffee table.

Hope flared in her face. 'And now you want me to get my father's signature.'

'I already have your father's signature, and my father's.'

Her mouth fell open.

'And Siena and Christian's,' he added. 'Obviously the pair of them didn't need much convincing—especially not after I presented them with the prospect of our children fighting over the damn necklace in twenty years' time.'

She waved a hand in front of her face. 'You have *my father's* signature?'

He unfolded the document and showed her.

She ran a finger over her father's name, and then his father's signature. 'How did you do this?'

'You did half the work, I believe. I made an appointment to see your father and told him what you wanted…told him I wanted it too. He said he would sign, just like that—no arguments, no wheeling or dealing—but I wanted more from him than just a signature.'

She glanced up. 'You wanted him to apologise to your father.'

Her perception shouldn't have surprised him. 'It was the only hope I had of getting my father to agree to all of this.'

She swallowed. 'How did my father take that?'

'He was quiet for a long time, stared out the window with his back to me, and then he told me you'd had a long talk with him and that he now knew it wasn't my father who'd rung Diana that day, but Tori.'

'And so he apologised to your father...in person?'

He nodded.

A breath whooshed out of her. 'Then I'm proud of him.' She glanced back at the signatures. 'Your father obviously accepted his apology, so I'm proud of him too.'

'I don't know what passed between them, and I suspect they'll never be best friends, but they'll present a united front when Christian and Siena officially announce their engagement. When they attend any future family functions, they'll pass a few polite pleasantries rather than veiled threats.'

She stared at him with wide eyes. 'You accomplished all of this?'

His heart started to hammer. She'd made herself vulnerable to him, had told him she loved him. He trusted her—would trust her with his life, his fortune and his heart—but saying it out loud scared the hell out of him.

Be braver, Nikos. She deserves it all.

'I love you, Marjorie.'

She stared, and then shook herself, as if she hadn't heard him properly.

'Before I met you I'd thought it impossible our families would ever stop fighting. But what I discovered is, what's truly impossible is living without you.'

She leaned forward, searching his face.

'I've never met anyone like you.' He pushed a strand of hair behind her ear. 'I've always liked how you look—my body always comes alive whenever we're in a room together—but it's your view of the world that captured my heart. You refuse to hold grudges and you believe the best of people, even when they give you no reason to, and you face your fears.

'You are so terrifyingly honest and—' he gulped '—I want to give you the world.' He hoped to God she still felt the same way about him. He traced a finger across her cheek. 'I realised that, if I had to move heaven and earth to be with you, then that was a small price to pay.'

Wonder crossed her face. She touched a hand to his cheek. 'You really love me?'

'Heart and soul.'

'You really trust me—a Mabel?'

Did she seriously think the feud held any

weight with him now? 'With my life, with my fortune and with my heart.'

MJ was almost afraid to breathe in case she should wake up and discover this was all a glorious dream. If it were a dream, she didn't want to wake up!

'Can I kiss you now?' His voice was a growl of need that raised every fine hair on her arms and had a shiver travelling a delicious path down her spine. In answer, she pressed her lips to his. Firm but gentle hands immediately caressed her face, lips caressing hers with a reverence that had tears pricking the backs of her eyes. Those lips firmed, and he deepened the kiss until she was breathless and clutching his shirt.

Heedless of the fact she would rumple his clothes, he pulled her into his lap. She ran her fingers over his face, down his neck and along his shoulders. *Mine.* This man belonged to her, body and soul.

'MJ.' Her name was dragged from his throat. 'Unless you have a lock on your office door...'

She contemplated continuing to play with fire—it felt like an age since she and Nikos had scaled the heights together—but there were still things to say. And, when they made love again—and she hoped that'd be soon—she didn't want any interruptions or intrusions. She wanted to focus on him and only him.

She gazed into his beloved face, touching her fingers to his jaw to bring his gaze back to hers. 'I love you, Nikos.'

Joy—pure, glorious and more freeing than anything she had ever experienced—poured into her in a crystal flow of brilliance and she saw the same emotion in his eyes. She couldn't temper her smile, and she didn't try. 'You did all of this for me.' She gestured at the document, now abandoned on the coffee table.

'I know I should say that I'm glad the feud is over for my father and grandfather's sakes, for Christian and Siena's sakes too, but all I cared about was making it possible for you to be in my life.'

Her heart leapt and swooped with his every word.

'When you walked out of my office after presenting me with the necklace…'

He broke off, shaking his head. 'I thought that was it. I thought there was no hope for us. But I couldn't forget you. I didn't want to forget you. I knew what we had was worth fighting for.'

'And so you applied yourself to finding a solution to an impossible problem.'

'Not impossible. Just challenging.'

She threw her head back and laughed for the sheer joy of it. 'You slayed my dragon, Nikos. You leave me breathless.'

'*Have* I slayed it?'

In answer, she reached across and signed the document.

'You didn't even read it! MJ, that's appalling business practice and...'

She touched her fingers to his lips. 'I trust you with my life, with my fortune and with my heart.'

His eyes darkened at her words. 'This isn't a proposal, Marjorie, because we've known each other properly for less than a month, but I want to build a life with you. I want to live with you, work beside you and be the father of your three children.'

Her heart pounded and her breath quickened. 'As it isn't a proposal, I won't say, *Yes, please*, and set a date for the wedding. But I will say I want all that and more.'

They kissed again. When they eased apart a long time later, she found herself laughing. 'Do you remember the day I stormed into your office and you asked what would happen if you kissed me? Well, I think you have your answer.'

His eyes gentled. 'I wouldn't have believed this possible back then.'

'Happy?' she whispered.

He trailed his fingers across her cheek. 'More than I ever thought possible.'

His edges blurred as her eyes misted over. 'Do you think we could ever find that little Greek island again? Do you think we could go there to hide away from the rest of the world once in a while? You could teach me to sail and we could go skinny-dipping.'

His smile speared straight into the centre of her. 'How about I buy it for you as a wedding present?'

She wrapped her arms around his waist and nestled against his chest, her lips curving up, her heart pounding in gratitude and happiness. 'Sounds perfect.'

He pulled her closer and pressed his lips to the top of her head. 'It does indeed.'

EPILOGUE

Christmas Day, three and a half years later...

'CAN I GET anyone more Christmas pudding?'

MJ's voice rose above the general hubbub. The long dining table was scattered with their now-empty plates and half-filled wine and water glasses that sparkled in the glow from the overhead chandelier. The discarded casings of the gaily coloured Christmas crackers lying abandoned between the dishes added a festive touch that made Nikos smile.

Much head shaking ensued, along with groans of how full everyone was and how they couldn't possibly fit another bite in. Nikos grinned at his wife presiding at the other end of the table. They'd married three years ago. They'd meant to wait until after Christian and Siena had tied the knot, but their siblings had yet to set a date.

MJ's words from three and a half years ago came to him now. *I'm thinking of all the Christmas dinners we'll share if Siena and Christian marry.* She'd evidently seen into the future, had seen all that was possible. He should never have doubted her or her vision for a moment.

Even now he found it hard to believe, had to pinch himself.

He was the luckiest man in the world.

Theirs was the luckiest family in the world.

'Why don't we adjourn to the living room?' he suggested, lifting his two-and-a-half-year-old son from his highchair. Paulo had arrived six months after his and MJ's wedding. 'The fire's been lit, MJ has organised nibbles and the good port has been brought up from the cellar.'

That last had grins spreading across his father's and grandfather's faces, while Graham rubbed his hands together in anticipation.

Siena came over, swooping in to lift Paulo from his father's arms and smacking a kiss to his plump cheek.

Paulo bounced his excitement and Nikos groaned. 'Lord, Siena, don't shake him up like you did last year.'

'Cross my heart. I've no intention of wearing my nephew's regurgitated dinner this year.'

He took nine-month-old Diana from MJ's arms. 'I hope you're not wearing yourself out.'

'Absolutely not.' She reached up and kissed his cheek. 'A fact I'll prove to you later when our guests have either gone home or retired for the night.'

Their gazes caught and clung. It wasn't what he'd meant, but her murmured words had licks of flame heating his blood. Their desire for each other hadn't waned in the last three-and-a-half years. If anything, it had grown. Eventually they blinked themselves back and followed everyone into the living room.

Once everyone was seated, staring lazily into the crackling flames of the fire, their beverage of choice clasped in their hands, Siena said, 'It's time to do MJ's gratitude list.'

On their very first Christmas together, when conversations had still been stilted among certain family members, MJ had insisted that everyone name three things they were grateful for that year. And she'd gone first.

She'd said she was grateful she'd found a once-in-a-lifetime love with Nikos; grateful that she and her family had weathered a tough time and had emerged stronger and closer than ever; and she'd said she was so proud to be a part of the Constantinos family, with its strong traditions and family ties.

But she hadn't stopped there. She'd said how much she loved living in the Grosvenor Square house, that she was grateful every day for her health and for having a job she loved. She'd said she felt blessed that both her families, old and new, were able to come together to share this very special day.

And a strange thing had happened as they'd listened to her. Rather than focusing on the negatives, everyone had made an effort to focus on the positives. They'd started listing things that had happened throughout the year that had brought them joy, and it had broken the ice. The Mabels and the Constantinoses had started to laugh and smile together.

MJ had been the force that had drawn them together, and that first Christmas she'd been the glue that held them together, because everyone had wanted to make amends to her. Her father for having lied to her, Siena for having caused her so much worry, Christian and Andreas because she'd revealed the truth that had mended their father-son relationship, and Vasillios because she'd given him back his beloved Joanie.

They'd exerted themselves that first year because they'd wanted MJ to have the Christmas of her dreams. And now, somehow, it was easy. Somewhere along the line, they'd become a family.

With his arm around MJ's shoulders and his daughter on his lap, Nikos listened as his flawed but wonderful family listed all the things they were grateful for.

'And now I have an announcement to make,' Graham said when everyone had had their turn. 'I've made the decision to retire. Andreas and I have several fishing and golf trips planned for the coming year, and I realised that's what I want to be doing at this time of my life—not going into the office every day. I'd like you to take over the reins of Mabel's, MJ. I can't think of anyone better to lead us into the future.'

MJ leapt up, her eyes shining and hands clasped beneath her chin. 'I'd *love* to step into your shoes. It'd be an honour, but only if you're sure.'

'I've never been surer of anything,' he said, kissing her cheek.

'As we're making announcements,' Andreas said, also rising to his feet, 'I've one of my own. I've decided to move in permanently with Graham.'

MJ's jaw dropped. She swung to stare at Nikos, who could only shake his head. When had his father decided this? She swung back. 'But this is your home!'

'Now don't take on, MJ,' the older man said, patting her arm. He'd moved out temporarily when his rooms were being refurbished and Graham had offered him lodgings in the Mabels' Knightsbridge residence. 'You have a growing family—' he glanced fondly at his grandchildren '—and Graham and I find we rub along together rather well. We have our bridge club and the wine society and...' He trailed off with a shrug. 'The arrangement suits us both.'

Not only was romance possible between their two families, but friendship apparently was too.

She bit her lip. 'Well, if you're sure, but you know there'll always be room for you here.'

'And at the Devon house,' Christian said, glancing at Siena.

Siena nodded, taking Christian's hand. 'As we seem to be making announcements, I guess we should tell you we've finally set a date. Christian and I are planning a summer wedding.'

Much hugging and excited chatter followed this news. Once they were all seated again, Nikos pressed his lips to MJ's temple. 'Are we going to share our news too?'

'You're having another baby!' Siena shrieked.

MJ happy-danced in her seat. 'I'm three months' pregnant and as healthy as a horse.'

More squeals. More hugging.

'So you're going to have the three babies you always wanted.' Siena sighed happily.

'Um, not quite,' MJ murmured, her eyes starting to dance.

Nikos straightened. Had she changed her mind? Did she want more children? They could have as many as she wanted!

'It appears I'm pregnant...*with twins.*'

He stared. 'Did you just say...?'

'Twins, Nikos.' She pointed at herself and Siena. 'It runs in the family. Tell me you're over the moon?'

With a whoop, he swept her up in his arms and swung her round. When he set her feet back on the ground, he kissed her with a thoroughness designed to leave her in no doubt of his feelings on the subject.

'Oh!' She clung to him, swaying slightly, her cheeks turning pink. 'Wow. So I guess that's a yes, then.'

Everyone laughed.

'Okay, that's it.' He settled her gently on the sofa with a cushion at her back and lifted her feet to a padded footstool. 'You're putting your feet up for the rest of the day. If you want anything, one of us will fetch it.'

Her father came across with a fresh glass of sparkling water. 'All of this…' he gestured around '…is because of you, my darling girl. I can't thank you enough.'

'Your father is right,' Andreas said, coming up beside him and handing her a plate of the choicest delicacies from among those on offer. 'Is there anything we can do to make things more perfect?'

MJ cocked her head, a smile spreading across those delectable lips. 'What would make things even more perfect was if we were to make a family group on the morrow to the Victoria and Albert Museum to see the Ananke necklace.'

That too had become a family tradition.

'Done!' the grandfathers said in unison.

'And then it'll be lunch at ours,' Graham said, raising an eyebrow at Andreas.

'Absolutely,' Andreas agreed.

'Oh, it sounds perfect.' MJ sighed. She tugged Nikos back down to the sofa beside her. 'Doesn't it?'

'The most perfect thing in the world,' he agreed, curving his arm around her and drawing her against him. She was the most perfect woman in the world, and she deserved every good thing the world had to offer. And he meant to make sure that she received it all—every single day.

* * * * *